The CAFÉ Club

4: JAIMINI AND THE WEB OF LIES

I pressed my knuckles into my cheeks to try and make the hot feeling go away. My heart was beating faster. "Please let me be totally wrong about this, God," I prayed, looking at the sky. I was beginning to feel like a really big fool. It looked horribly as though Dom was carrying out the joke of the century on me – telling me all sorts of stupid lies to get out of seeing me again. But why? And why did Carl tell Luce to make sure I'd be in the café because Dom wanted me there?

Also in the Café Club series by Ann Bryant

Have you read?
Go For It, Fen!
Leah Discovers Boys
Luce and the Weird Kid

Look out for:
Andy the Prisoner

The CAFE Club

4: JAIMINI AND THE WEB OF LIES

Ann Bryant

Hippo

Scholastic Children's Books,
Commonwealth House, 1–19 New Oxford Street,
London WC1A 1NU, UK
a division of Scholastic Ltd
London ~ New York ~ Toronto ~ Sydney ~ Auckland

First published by Scholastic Ltd, 1996

Copyright © Ann Bryant, 1996

ISBN 0 590 13427 2

Typeset by TW Typesetting, Midsomer Norton, Avon

Printed by Cox & Wyman Ltd, Reading, Berks.

For Howard and Mahin

Chapter 1

Hi! I'm Jaimini. There are six of us altogether – six friends, that is. We're all thirteen and we all go to Cableden Comprehensive School which is a great school to go to. Let's start with Luce, the crazy one. Sometimes at night I lie awake and stare at the ceiling and say, "Dear God, please give me one good reason why I've got that weird girl for my best friend. We have hardly anything in common and she positively exasperates me at times."

Then I wait for his answer, and it's almost as though he's reeling off the reasons, because at least six pop into my head all at once – she's all the things I sometimes wish *I* was; she's warm and generous, she's happy, wild and impulsive. But most of all, I'm *her* best friend and she says that will never change. Her real name is Lucy Edmunson but she's been Luce to us lot since the year dot. She's got a wild mass of strawberry-blonde curls, green eyes and freckles. She also wears ridiculously fancy earrings.

Fen, the ambitious one, started our Café Club going. Her real name is Fenella Brooks and she's got an aunt, Jan, who runs a local café. Fen finally got Jan to agree to let all six of us work at the café on a rota basis, from Monday to Saturday. Of course, it's only for a couple of hours after school, but whoever does Saturday gets longer, which is great because that means more money, and we all need money, let's face it! Fen is really thin and wiry with shoulder-length brown hair and a face that shows determination.

Her best friend is called Tash, the peacemaker. Tash is short for Natasha Johnston and she is a very sensible, reliable girl with an open smile and twinkly brown eyes. It's impossible to dislike Tash. She is very pretty and has lovely thick dark hair in a sort of bob.

Then there's Leah, the musician. She's got beautiful long blonde hair that Luce says she'd kill for. But then Luce also says she'd kill for *my* hair, which is long, straight and black. Basically, Luce would like long straight hair, as you may have gathered.

Anyway, back to Leah. Leah Bryan is her full name and she's got a lovely serene face with very milky skin. She's the kind of girl you look twice at – if not three times! She doesn't realize she's that good-looking, and neither does she give herself any credit for being a really talented violinist and pianist. She thinks anyone could play as well as she does as long as they practise, but it's not true. She was born with some kind of gift.

Leah's best friend is Andy, the daring one. Andy is amazing. I mean, *really* amazing. She's the smallest of us all – petite is a good word to describe her, because Andy is actually half French. Her real name is Agnès, which is a French name that you pronounce Ann-yes, but we've always called her Andy – Andy Sorrell. She's got very dark cropped hair, dark eyes and skin, and a thin face with lovely bone structure. Her colouring is the nearest of all to mine.

You see, my mum is white and my dad is black, so I'm sort of half-way between the two, which is another thing Luce says she'd die for! Every so often she grabs me by the shoulders and says, "Look at me, Jaimes." (That's my nickname, short for Jaimini, which you pronounce Jay-m-nee, by the way.) "Look at me, Jaimes," then she stares into my eyes and calls out to whoever happens to be within earshot, "Look at this! You won't believe this! It's impossible to tell where Jaimini's pupils finish and the rest of her eyes start! You're supposed to be the brainy one, Jaimes, you can't be beautiful as well!" Then she breaks into "All things bright and beautiful," but generally only manages the first two lines before we all crack up laughing, because she makes a big thing of pointing down at the top of my head while she sings the first line, then she points to herself for "All creatures great…" and to Andy on "…and small"!

So, you may have gathered from all that that I'm supposed to be the brainy one. I know it's meant as a compliment, but somehow it just makes me feel boring. You have to be very careful round here not to be called "square", which means really swotty, always studying hard and getting good marks, and appearing to enjoy work. It can be quite a problem because I *do* enjoy work most of the time, which is handy because I sometimes find myself doing six lots of homework!

Andy often jokes and says, "Jaimes, you're lucky, you've got the easy bit – providing us with the basic facts. It's the embellishment that's the creative bit. It takes real imagination to make enough little adjustments so that the six final versions don't resemble each other at all, and even the most suspicious teacher won't notice we've copied off you!"

Good old Andy. She probably copies my work the least of any of them. But today at school she was desperate to get my help, only in a different way this time.

"Jaimes, please, please, *please* can we swap days at the café this week? It's supposed to be my turn today, but I'd forgotten I promised I'd look after Sebastien after school. Mum's not getting back till quite late." (Sebastien is Andy's one-year-old brother.) I would love to look after him but he doesn't know me well enough.

"Lucky thing!" I said, with feeling. "Yeah, OK. I haven't got anything after school. I'll do it for you."

"You're a gem, Jaimes. Thanks," she said warmly.

All through the last lesson of the afternoon I was thinking about the café. It makes you feel so grown up and also I really like Fen's aunt Jan.

"Jaimini, are you with us?" Mr Waring, the maths teacher, interrupted my daydreams.

"Oh, sorry."

"Well?"

"Um… I didn't hear the question."

"Oh, dear me, you're going to have to apply yourself one hundred per cent if you're to go to Finsbury Leighton, you know."

When Mr Waring said that I nearly shot out of my chair.

"Finsbury Leighton! But I'm not going there!"

His eyes darted from side to side before settling back on me. "Well, you never know," he said, trying to make light of it, then he coughed as though gathering himself together after a big gaffe. "The answer I was looking for was 'corresponding angles', Jaimini."

"Oh, yes," I replied, though I hadn't a clue what he was on about because I couldn't stop thinking about what he'd said about Finsbury Leighton. It was more the fact that he'd said it in the first place. I mean, why mention the school at all unless there had been some sort of talk about my going there? I suddenly wished I was going straight home and not to the café after school. I just wanted to check that Mum and Dad didn't have any silly ideas in their heads about me changing schools.

Going out of the main doors at quarter to four I saw Andy and Leah chatting nineteen to the dozen.

"Hi, you two."

"Hiya! You look worried. What's the matter?" Andy asked, and both of them frowned and walked along with me, one on either side.

"Oh, just something Mr Waring said." They were looking at me, waiting for me to go on. "...about me going to another school."

"No!" said Andy, stopping suddenly in her tracks which made the three girls behind us go careering into her.

"Sorry," they mumbled, because people always apologize to Andy as she looks so little and delicate. Andy, however, didn't even notice. There was a decidedly stubborn look on her face as if to say, "I'm not going another step further until you reassure me that Mr Waring was talking total rubbish!"

"Nobody's said anything to me," I said, grabbing Andy's arm so we could get moving again instead of blocking everyone's way.

"So, why did he mention it?" Leah wanted to know.

"Your guess is as good as mine. As soon as I get home I'll quiz Mum about it."

"Yeah, then phone me," Andy insisted.

"OK, but it'll be after six. I'm on duty at the café, remember?" I warned her as we parted ways.

"Hello... Anybody there?" Kevin the chef joked as I walked in through the back door of the café to the kitchen, where he was making quiches. I must have been miles away, deep in my own thoughts, because Kevin had to wave his arms in front of my face to bring me back down to earth.

"Sorry, Kevin," I said with a smile. No matter how worried or sad or cross or anything else you feel when you go to work, Kevin always cheers you up.

"Hi, pet," Jan greeted me in her usual way. "We're not too busy at the moment but I could do with a load of paper serviettes being folded and trays being wiped, and I think

Kevin wanted you to scrub some vegetables."

I put one of the white aprons from the drawer on over my black school uniform, and set to work on the trays.

"Hi, Jaimini," Mark said, as he grabbed a full tray and went back into the café. Mark is seventeen and really nice. He's training to teach martial arts when he's not working at the café.

"What's new, then?" asked Kevin.

"Finsbury Leighton School," I answered automatically.

"Never heard of it," said Kevin.

"I wish I hadn't either," I told him, tight-lipped.

"Posh, is it?" Kevin wanted to know.

"You could say that," I smiled.

"Wouldn't suit you then."

I took that as a compliment as Kevin was grinning inanely into his cooking.

We worked away in silence for a while, apart from Kevin's occasional bursts of singing which are really amusing to listen to. He never sings for more than three or four seconds and it's always really loud and tuneless with all the wrong words, then it suddenly stops and he carries on working … until the next little outburst.

Today he was treating me to extracts from *The Sound of Music*. I couldn't stop giggling when he suddenly sang, "Grumpety grump, sang the lonely goatherd…" Then he yodelled like an opera singer with hiccups!

"You know what the answer is, don't you?" he asked me out of the blue. I didn't know what he was talking about except that it was obviously something serious because he had stopped whisking and was looking at me very gravely.

"The answer to what?" I asked, getting a sudden flashback to Mr Waring talking about corresponding angles.

"The answer is to pretend you're not as bright as you really are," he said.

"You mean…"

"I mean, if you want to stay at Cableden Comp., you'd better not work so hard."

I kept thinking about what Kevin had said

while I was cleaning and chopping vegetables and folding napkins. It was a good idea of his, because to get into Finsbury Leighton you had to pass an entrance exam, and if your school doesn't think you'll pass it, they advise your parents against your taking it.

"Lots of customers all of a sudden," announced Jan, flying through the swing doors at seventy miles per hour. "Could you take orders from tables three, four and five, Jaimini?"

I grabbed my pad and pencil and went through to the café. Two girls were sitting with their mothers at table three. I approached them with a big smile and said, "Hello, are you ready to order yet?"

They were all looking at the menus. The two girls looked about my age or a bit older. They glanced at me, then carried on studying their menus. One of the mothers looked up and said, "We're not quite ready yet," in rather an impatient voice as though I were interrupting her concentration or something.

"That's all right. I'll come back in a moment," I said as politely as I could, reminding myself that the customer is always right even if you would like to strangle them. I then went to table four where four women whom I'd seen in the café before greeted me cheerfully and launched straight into their orders. I was half-way through when I realized that one of the ladies from table three was trying to attract my attention.

"Waitress, excuse me," she called in a rather affected voice. "We're actually ready now."

"I'll be with you in half a minute," I said, but not too loudly because Jan is very strict about not calling out across the café.

Just before I turned back to the table four ladies, I distinctly saw the two women at table three roll their eyes at each other and one of them heaved a big sigh as if she was fed up with putting up with poor service or something. I quickly finished off the order I was doing and went back to their table.

"Right…" My pen was poised.

"A pot of tea for two and two hot chocolates."

"Two teas, two hot chocolates," I repeated as I wrote it down.

"No, a *pot* of tea for two, not two teas," the second lady, who was wearing a navy blue suit and a lot of pink lipstick, corrected me. She smiled but it wasn't a proper smile.

I didn't say anything because I was afraid that if I opened my mouth I might say something awful like, "Right, madam, and would you like the tea in a cup or all over your tight, new perm?"

One of the girls was nudging her mother.

"Oh, yes," said the woman, "and what gateaux do you have?"

"The gateaux are over there by the counter. You can choose whichever one you like."

The girls got up and went over to choose. They were wearing maroon pleated skirts and jumpers, pink and blue shirts, and I could see their grey blazers hanging over the backs of their chairs. What a hideous uniform, I thought. I wonder what school that is?

I cut them slices of gateau, then went to take table five's order before rushing back to the kitchen to give Kevin the top copy for the three orders.

"What does FLS stand for?" Jan asked me in a whisper as we stood side by side doing drinks at the counter.

"No idea," I told her, whizzing away with my pot of tea for two, and two hot chocolates.

It wasn't until at least an hour later when I was washing up that I felt my face turn pale as realization dawned on me … FLS – Finsbury Leighton School!

"Jan," I demanded, swinging suddenly away from the washing-up, "why did you ask me what those letters stood for?"

She frowned. "Oh, *those* letters. FLS. It was written on those girls' blazers. I just wondered what school they were from."

"I don't think a blazer would suit you, Jaimini," Kevin called out above the sound of his food processor. He winked and grinned as he said it. It always amazed me how Kevin managed to hear everything that was going on, even though he often gave the impression he was completely wrapped up in whatever he was doing.

"What's he talking about?" Jan asked me,

jerking her head in Kevin's direction. I didn't answer.

"And why are you looking so intently into thin air while dripping frothy water all over my floor?" she went on.

I quickly turned back to the sink. There was no need to answer because Jan had rushed off again, leaving me with the ghastly reminder of a school I didn't want to go to.

The moment I could get away I hurried home and decided on the way that I wouldn't mention the school straight away. I'd wait till Dad got in, then if neither Mum nor Dad said anything at all about Finsbury Leighton, I'd ask them outright.

Mum was ironing as I walked into the kitchen and she looked really excited about something.

Oh, no! This is it! I thought. She's about to tell me they've decided to send me to Finsbury Leighton, and she obviously thinks I'm going to be thrilled down to my DM's.

"Guess what!" Mum said, putting the iron

down and giving me her undivided attention.

"What?" I asked softly.

"I'm thinking of going back to work," she said.

"Oh!"

I nearly fell over, it was such an unexpected announcement.

"You mean, you're going back to nursing?"

"Yes. It's not definite yet, but I thought perhaps nights."

"Nights? Why?"

"Well, the pay's very good and it would mean I wouldn't miss out on seeing you after school…"

"Oh … well, that's great."

I didn't really know what else to say, because as far as I knew, the only reason Mum hadn't gone back to work before is because for years she's been trying to get pregnant. I'm an only child and I'd love to have a brother or sister. Perhaps Mum had given up the idea of having another baby for some reason or other, because I was certain that if she *did* have another baby she'd want to be at home with it, as she'd been waiting and hoping for so many years. Anyway, at least for the moment I didn't have to worry about Finsbury Leighton.

"How was your day?" Mum asked. She'd packed up the ironing board and was tidying the kitchen.

"Fine," I said noncommittally, as I began to help her.

Mum loves tidying things up. That's why our house is so neat. Even my bedroom's quite tidy. In fact, sometimes I feel so embarrassed about it being in such order when Luce's is so chaotic, that I deliberately chuck a cushion on the floor and scatter a few books and cassettes around the place, so that Luce feels more at home when she comes here.

I love my bedroom. It's my very favourite place to be. I haven't got a proper ceiling light, just a desk lamp, a bedside lamp and a wall light which make the room really atmospheric. It's medium-sized with a beautiful patchwork quilt on the bed. The girls made the quilt, with Mum's help, as a birthday present for me. I think it's the best present

I've ever had. I know exactly which squares are from whom, because they sewed their initial into every square they did, just in a corner. Because Luce and Leah have the same initial, Luce made her L's bigger, but I would have known which was which anyway, because Leah's L's are much neater and straighter than Luce's – rather like their hair really! I had one further surprise from them for that birthday. Pinned to one of their own squares I found a friendship bracelet from each of them, which I've been wearing ever since.

Also in my bedroom there are six candle holders with different coloured scented candles in each, a joss-stick holder with holes for five joss-sticks, three mobiles of suns, moon, stars and little brass bells, various little dishes full of pot pourri, a rag rug and some Indian scarves hanging from my wardrobe and bookcase. I collect mobiles and candles and things like that. Mum says I'm a born-again hippie!

Anyway, back to the kitchen. I decided to elaborate on my day a bit, in order to find out whether Mum had any plans to send me to Finsbury Leighton, and also to give Cableden a big vote of confidence for her benefit.

"Actually, I had a brilliant day. Mr Waring is such a good maths teacher. In fact, it's only because of him that I like maths so much. Luckily, he'll still be my maths teacher next year, too."

I paused and glanced at her to see how she was taking it so far, but her hair was hanging over her face so I couldn't tell. I decided to carry on a bit with something that I just thought of that was completely made up.

"Oh, and great news! Leah is coming into my work group for maths and geography, and Tash is joining me for science. I'm really pleased because I know I see the girls at break, but it's not the same as being in the same work groups." Again I paused.

"Not Luce then?" she asked.

"No, we're only together for music, PE, drama and PSE."

"Well, never mind. When you're really good friends with someone, it doesn't matter if you're not always in the same class. In fact, it doesn't really matter if you're not even in the same school. After all, there are always the weekends and holidays."

I could feel my heart starting to beat faster. This sounded horribly like a lead into some dreadful announcement. I wasn't about to make it easy for Mum because there was no way I was going to any other school but Cableden, and she'd better know that.

"Weekends and holidays aren't enough, I'm afraid," I said firmly. "You see, your school is the most central part of your life. Well, for us six it is. That – and the café, of course."

"Hmm."

"What do you mean 'hmm'?" I suddenly snapped at her. She didn't answer. "I *know* what you mean, anyway," I told her, raising my voice. That made her look at me properly. We faced each other across the kitchen with mounting anger hanging between us.

"Mr Waring let it slip about Finsbury Leighton, and I'll tell you right now, just in case you have any ideas about sending me there, I'm not going and that's that!"

"I'm not prepared to discuss it till your father gets home, then we'll talk about it sensibly, thank you very much."

"There's nothing to discuss. I'm not going."

Mum didn't answer so I went out of the back door, slamming it, then headed for Luce's higgledy-piggledy house.

On the way I could feel tears pricking at the back of my eyes, which really irritated me because my eyes are so big that the tears fall out more easily than they do with average-sized eyes. So by the time I was standing at Luce's back door I'd got three sodden tissues in my hand and there were two more big tears about to roll.

Chapter 2

"**O**h, Jaimes, whatever's the matter?" Luce asked as she opened the door. She put her arm round me and steered me down to the bottom of the garden. "We'll go in the greenhouse. It's the only place you can get any peace round here. The twins are making up a football song which involves whirling those noisy rattle things round their heads and clapping loudly in between."

I sputtered out a giggle in the middle of my tears, because Luce's twin brothers, Leo and Tim, aged eight, were continually doing something interesting in their lives, and whatever it was, it invariably got on Luce's nerves.

We sat down in the greenhouse and I related to Luce the conversation I'd just had with Mum, and also what Mr Waring had said. Then I remembered what Kevin had suggested in the café, and told Luce that too.

"Kevin reckoned that if I didn't work so hard they might change their minds."

"Kevin's a genius," Luce announced, clapping her hands together and looking radiant. "It's so simple! Get dumbo marks in all subjects, and there's no way they'll think you're capable of coping at a school like Finsbury Leighton, which is supposed to be so swotty."

I must have been frowning because Luce carried on trying to convince me with her argument. "I mean, you mustn't do it suddenly or anything, but just gradually show that you're concentrating less, and of course, your attitude has got to change completely."

The uncertainty I felt about whether I could do it convincingly must have shown on my face.

"It's such a shame you can't follow me

around school for a while. You'd soon get the hang of staring out of the window, forgetting to hand your homework in and asking the teacher to repeat something three times because you can't write it down quickly enough."

I grinned at Luce's description of herself. "Oh, come on, you're not *that* bad."

"Want a bet?"

When I went home about an hour later, I was feeling much better. After all, if I spoke calmly and sensibly to Mum and Dad about my reasons for not wanting to go to Finsbury Leighton, they would probably forget the whole idea.

It's important to present Dad with a very sensible argument because he's got no patience with people who jump into things with both feet and no thought. I quite admire my dad, really. He's got a good job in computers and he's very brainy indeed, but not at all boring.

He's tall and thin, but also very strong because he did a lot of rock climbing and other sports when he was younger. I think he's good-looking but it's difficult to judge when it's your own dad. I asked Luce what she thought once, and she said, "Jaimes, your dad is rather too old for me, but believe me, if I were thirty years older, I'd say he was drop dead gorgeous!" So that gave me a pretty good idea!

The only trouble is that Mum and Dad are both very strict with me. That's one reason why I wish I'd got a brother or sister, because then their strictness would be shared out between two children rather than me copping the whole lot!

"Jaimini was asking about Finsbury Leighton, Rick," Mum said to Dad when we were eating later. (Rick is short for Ricardo, by the way. I already mentioned that Dad's half Italian and half Ethiopian, didn't I?) "Apparently Mr Waring said something about the school in the maths lesson."

"I reckon it's the perfect school for a girl like you," Dad said, looking at me with a mixture of enthusiasm and don't-you-dare-think-otherwise-ness.

"I'm not going," I told him stubbornly. The moment the words were out of my mouth I regretted them, because I'd agreed with myself that I would tackle the conversation sensibly and calmly, and here I was blowing it at the first base.

"I can assure you, you *are* going. The decision has been made."

"But I don't want to leave my friends."

"You won't be leaving them. You'll merely be going to a different school where presumably you'll make even more friends."

"It won't be the same. I wouldn't be happy anywhere but Cableden."

"I've never heard you singing Cableden's praises before," Dad commented drily.

"It's not just the school, it's my friends and all we do… At least the Café Club's after school," I said, thinking out loud.

"Well, I'm afraid that will have to go as far as you're concerned."

"What!" I screeched, standing up and knocking my plate into my glass, which toppled over. Mum stared at the patch of water slowly spreading wider and wider, as Dad and I stared at each other, eyes flashing.

"I am *never* giving up the Café Club," I told him, in one of my rare moments of determination and anger.

"You will do as you're told, young lady," he snapped back at me.

"You can't make me," I retorted, feeling more tears about to start flowing.

"Can't I?" he answered ominously.

That's when I fled up to my room and lay face down on the bed feeling like an eight-year-old again.

The next morning break, down at our favourite spot on the netball courts, I broke my awful news to the others.

"You can't go," Fen said decisively, "and that's that!"

"I wish it were as simple as that," I said with a sigh.

"Kevin suggested she drops her standards a bit so nobody thinks she's good enough," Luce explained, "and I agree with him."

"When is the entrance exam?" Leah wanted to know.

"Or put another way, how long have you got to show what a lazy, good-for-nothing you've become?" Andy asked with a grin.

"I don't know. I'm not speaking to my parents at the moment. You see, the very worst thing of all is that Dad says I won't be able to work at the café any more."

"Oh, that's terrible," said Leah and Tash simultaneously.

"Let's go and get a few details about it off Mr Waring," Fen suggested. "Come on."

So we all trooped up to the staffroom and knocked on the door. It was Mrs Merle, everybody's favourite teacher, who answered.

"My goodness, what a deputation," she said, smiling round. "What can I do for you?"

"Could we speak to Mr Waring, please?" I asked.

A moment later he appeared and looked even more taken aback at the sight of six of us than Mrs Merle had.

"Mum and Dad told me about Finsbury

Leighton," I launched in, "and I was just wondering when the entrance exam is?"

"It's next Thursday, but I shouldn't worry about it. As long as you work as well as usual you'll be absolutely fine…"

"Right, thank you," I said quietly.

Nobody spoke till we were back outside again. Then Luce took control.

"OK, Jaimes, what lessons have you got for the rest of today?"

"Double science, French and history," I told her, "…and a test in science."

"Perfect. Now listen carefully. You answer every question wrongly in the science test – and I mean every single one. You speak Italian in the French lesson, and stare out of the window all through history. Then you go straight to the café and sit there sipping Coke until it shuts. (I'm on duty by the way.) Next you walk home very slowly, calling in at my place on the way, then when you get home you tell your parents exactly where you've been, and when they blow a fuse and say, 'Why weren't you at home doing homework?'

you say, 'I did it in the library at lunchtime. It only took me five minutes because I decided not to bother to do three pages of A4, like the teacher asked, I just did half a page because English bores me silly!' Got all that?"

By the end of her speech we were all falling about laughing. In fact we were still laughing as we split up for lessons and Luce was giving me last minute tips, like, "If you get bored with staring out of the window, try examining your hair for split ends."

I handed my science test in at the end of the lesson with a shaky hand and wobbly knees. I'd deliberately got nearly everything wrong and I knew Mr Osbourne wouldn't understand what on earth had come over me.

The girls were delighted when I told them at lunchtime.

"See you after school, then," Luce said after lunch. "We'll walk down to the café together and you can tell me all about how badly you did in French and history." She beamed excitedly.

"Oh, I've just remembered something," I

told Luce. "Mum said there was someone she wanted me to meet after school. I've no idea who because I'm not talking to her so I couldn't ask."

"Just ignore that," Luce said with a wave of her hand. "You're coming to the café with me, I'm afraid." I had to smile at Luce's authoritative manner. We parted ways and I decided to phone Mum up quickly and tell her I was helping Luce out at the café. That way she wouldn't be worried about me, but she'd know I was still cross.

There was no reply but the answerphone was on, so I left a message saying, "It's me. I'm going to the café after school. See you later. Bye." Then off I went to stare out of the window, check my hair for split ends and speak Italian. That's not quite as ridiculous as it sounds because of my dad being half Italian, which makes me a quarter Italian!

"How did you get on?" Luce asked, as she and the others clustered around me outside the school gates.

"I think I'm doing really well," I told them all.

"You mean really badly," Tash corrected me.

"Yes, really badly," I agreed with a laugh.

A few minutes later, Luce and I went in through the back door of the café and I leaned against the Aga and chatted to Becky and Kevin for a few moments. Becky, Mark and Debra all work part time at the café. Debra does the most but we hardly ever see her because she finishes at three o'clock. All three of them are just as nice as Jan. We're lucky to be able to work in such a friendly place.

"Hello, pets," Jan said to Luce and me. "Your mum's in there already, Jaimini," she went on.

"Mum!" I squawked, looking at Luce in horror. "What's she doing here?"

"Oh, she seemed to be expecting you," Jan said. "She's got someone with her for you to meet. You'd better go and join her, hadn't you?"

Reluctantly I entered the café, aware of Luce

peering over my shoulder. There at table six sat Mum, one of the girls I'd seen in Finsbury Leighton uniform the other day and two boys whom I'd never set eyes on in my life but who were very good-looking indeed. Luce obviously thought so too because as the swing door swung back, I distinctly heard her whisper, "Nice one, Bren."

My mother's name is Brenda and Luce is always calling her Bren, which Mum says makes her feel young. Mum is quite fair with wavy shoulder-length hair and blue eyes. All my colouring comes from my dad. I approached the table slowly and as soon as Mum saw me she jumped up.

"Oh, here she is," she said to the girl. "Jaimini, this is Clarissa Bede. I met Clarissa's mother by chance at the Flower Festival and she mentioned that Clarissa goes to Finsbury Leighton, so I thought it would be nice for you to meet someone who already goes there. This is Jaimini, Clarissa."

All the while Mum had been talking I'd been aware of Clarissa's stare of amazement.

People always react like that when they see Mum and me together for the first time. It's because they can't work out how two such different-looking people could possibly be mother and daughter.

I tried to smile at Clarissa but my mouth didn't really feel like moving so it must have come across as a very odd smile. I turned to the attractive boy beside her, who like Clarissa had dark eyes and skin, though not as dark as mine, of course. I guessed he would be a year older than me.

"This is Dominic, Clarissa's brother," Mum explained. This time my mouth broke into a very wide smile without any effort, and I think it would have stayed there too, if I hadn't felt Luce nudging me while smoothing her hand backwards and forwards over the tablecloth rather unnecessarily. I know Luce, and she'd just come to get a better view of the good-looking boys, and possibly even an introduction.

"Um ... this is Lucy Edmunson," I obliged her.

"And this is Carl, Dominic's friend," Mum said, so that everyone knew everyone else's name. I sat down and tried not to giggle as Luce fussed around the table, moving the salt and pepper slightly to the left, the menu slightly to the right.

Carl and Luce couldn't help stealing little looks at each other. I felt quite relieved it was Carl and not Dominic who she was interested in, because when Luce sets her sights on someone, no one else gets a look in! I've never been interested in boys before, but something told me that that was about to change.

"Do you go to Finsbury Leighton too, Dominic?" I asked as casually as I could.

"Yeah – and it's Dom," he answered, sounding as cool as a cucumber. I tried to rearrange my sitting position so I'd look a bit cooler too, but it wasn't working very well. I felt really gangly and stupid.

"Are you going to take our orders, Luce?" Mum asked pleasantly, but with a slight hint that Luce should stop fiddling.

"No ... yes ... yes, of course..." cried Luce,

a bit over-enthusiastically. She rummaged in her apron pocket and brought out her pad and pencil, but still her eyes seemed to be paying more attention to the sandy-haired Carl than to her note pad.

When our drinks came I was almost scared to drink mine in case I dribbled or something. I knew that was a ridiculous thought, but I wanted to be absolutely perfect in Dom's eyes. I also wanted to know as much as possible about him, but on the other hand I didn't want to appear too keen, so I focused my attention on Clarissa and Finsbury Leighton, which delighted Mum, of course.

"It's a super school," Clarissa informed me confidently. "Super" is a word my friends and I never ever use, so Clarissa lost a point straight away. "And the teachers are really great," she added, enthusiastically.

At that moment Luce returned for the third time and started sweeping the floor with a brush and dustpan about half a metre from Carl's chair. Then she leaned over to me and said. "Jaimini, where did you put the cooling racks yesterday? Only Kevin wants them and we can't find them."

I was about to protest and say that I'd never set eyes on any cooling racks before in my life, when I realized that Luce's eyes were boring into mine and her mouth was set in a fine line. I got the hint.

"I'll show you," I said, jumping up and following her through to the kitchen.

The moment we were through to the other side of that swing door, Luce spun round to me with an ecstatic look on her face and said, "Oh, Jaimes, aren't they gorgeous!"

I smiled and agreed that they were nice-looking.

"You've just gotta fix it for me to see that lovely Carl again, Jaimes. Get really friendly with that what's-'er-name."

"Clarissa?"

"Yes, Clarissa with the 'really great' teachers! I ask you, Jaimes, how can a teacher be really great? Let's face it, a teacher's a teacher. It's Saturday tomorrow. See if we can meet them in here – without Bren, of course."

"Too much chatter and not enough work, Lucy," Jan commented with disapproval.

"I'll phone you later," I whispered as I slipped quickly back into the café. I couldn't resist looking straight at our table and I was glad I did because Dom's eyes were on the kitchen door and he gave me a lovely smile when he saw it was me.

"We were just talking about clubs," Mum told me as I sat down.

"You can do practically anything you want," Clarissa told me, palms up, shoulders raised. "There's even an origami club!"

Dom whispered something to Carl behind his hand and both boys sniggered.

"Shut up, Dom," Clarissa told her brother with a scowl.

"So you work here too, do you?" Carl asked me.

"Yeah," I answered feeling myself positively glowing with street cred.

I felt certain one of them would want to know more, but Carl just said, "Oh," and that was the end of the conversation.

I bet Mum's primed them, I thought. I bet she's said, "Jaimini will have to give up the café job, and she's a bit upset about it."

But I was wrong because it was Mum herself who carried on with the subject. "There are six of them and they do one day each after school and all afternoon on a Saturday."

"On a rota basis, you know," I put in.

"I sometimes help in the tuck shop in morning break," Clarissa told me, as though that was just the same as working in a café.

"Do you get paid?" I couldn't resist asking.

She shook her head and quickly changed the subject. "When's your half term?"

"Next week," I told her.

"Oh, we go back next Thursday. We broke up yesterday. That's why we were in the café even though it was only just after four o'clock."

"What time does your school normally finish then?"

"Well, there's always some club or other after school till five and most people stay on till six and do their prep at school."

So that's why Dad had said the Café Club

would have to go. I felt a moment of panic rise to the surface again, then I tried to tell myself calmly that the battle was far from over. By the time I'd finished with Mum and Dad they wouldn't make me go to Finsbury Leighton. And even if the worst came to the very worst, nobody could make me go to clubs after school. I'd be able to work at the café at least once a week.

"Which one of your friends is working here tomorrow?" Clarissa suddenly asked.

"Um … Leah."

"There's quite a good atmosphere here. I might come back tomorrow afternoon," Dom said casually, which made my heart leap. Mum beamed happily. I expect she was thinking, "This is all turning out very well. How clever of me to introduce Jaimini to Clarissa's brother. Now she'll definitely want to go to Finsbury Leighton." Well, she was wrong about that, but I had to admit, I didn't feel *quite* so strongly opposed to it as I had done.

Mum paid the bill and we all walked home together to our house. Mrs Bede arrived not long after and stayed and had a cup of tea with Mum. Us four had already got into the "Game of Life", and as time went on I found myself liking Clarissa more and more. She lived about a mile from our house and said she didn't mind biking over the next day.

"Why don't you two come too?" I said to Dom and Carl as casually as I could, "and we could all go down to the café?"

"Yeah, OK," Dom said, but Clarissa was wrinkling her nose and I could tell she didn't want her brother around.

"Or Jaimini could come to our house," suggested Mrs Bede.

"That would be nice. Thanks," I said quickly, because that way I was guaranteed a sighting of Dom.

So the following afternoon at two o'clock I biked over to Clarissa's house, and nearly fell off my bike as I went up their long drive, partly because pea shingle is a very difficult surface to ride on, but also because I was shocked at the length of the drive and the enormous house at the end of it.

"So you found it OK?" said a familiar voice, which made my stomach flutter.

"Ye-es, no problem," I answered Dom, who was fiddling with his bike chain and had oil all over his hands. He wiped them on his pale blue jeans and gave me a smile that made my stomach have another funny turn. So this is what it feels like to fancy someone, I thought. No wonder Luce raves about it all the time and fancies every other boy she meets.

"Clarissa's in the house. She's got another friend with her."

"Oh right, I'll go in then."

"I'll show you the way."

I was glad it was such a big house because then it would take Dom all the longer to show me the way. As it happened Clarissa came running to the door to meet me, and Dom turned and went away.

"Hi, Jaimini, this is Sarah Rutter, my friend from school."

Sarah and I greeted each other shyly. She had very red hair, freckles and a big grin.

"We were just wondering if your friend Lucy would like to come over too," Clarissa asked, and I suddenly felt really guilty because I'd forgotten all about Luce. I'd promised to ring her after she got home from work yesterday. Poor Luce.

"Oh, yes, that'd be great," I said. "Can I give her a ring?"

Luce was not very pleased with me, I could tell. She was extremely quiet on the phone, but she did agree to come over to Clarissa's, and I said I'd go back half-way to meet her. This was a good idea for two reasons. One – it would give me the chance to apologize to Luce without the others all listening, and two – I'd get to go past Dom twice more!

Chapter 3

"Off already?" Dom said, as he emerged from the shed and saw me getting back on my bike.

"I'm going to meet Luce. You know – my friend who was working in the café yesterday. I'm bringing her here. We'll be back in about quarter of an hour."

"Oh. Right."

Afterwards when I was riding along I felt stupid. I mean, there was no need to tell him when we'd be back, was there? Now he'd think I was too keen. Fancy explaining all my pathetic little arrangements. I bet Andy wouldn't have done that – or Leah – or any of them, except perhaps Luce. I couldn't under-stand what was coming over me. I'd never imagined that one boy could have such a strong effect as to make you dithery and silly. Dom hadn't shown any interest whatsoever when I'd said I was coming back. I resolved to be much more sensible and distant from that moment on.

So when Luce and I crunched up the drive fifteen minutes later to the accompaniment of rapturous cries from Luce, I kept my eyes straight ahead and went past the shed as fast as I could. I needn't have bothered. There was no sign of Dom anywhere. He'd probably gone out.

I rang the bell and Clarissa and Sarah appeared at the door. I introduced Luce and Sarah, then we all went up to Clarissa's room and stood there tongue-tied for a bit.

"Do you like cooking?" Clarissa finally asked.

I said "yes" straight away because I thought there was more chance of coming across Dom if we were anywhere but Clarissa's bedroom.

So we went down to the kitchen and started going through recipe books to try and find something very sickly and interesting-looking to make.

In the end we decided to mix up two different cake recipes and see how it turned out. Luce was still rather quiet even though she'd forgiven me for not phoning her, so when we were crouching down together by the oven and the other two were making a lot of noise with the electric mixer, I asked her if she was OK.

"I was kinda hoping Carl would be here," she confided, sounding embarrassed, which is most unusual for Luce. Then, talk about miracles, the mixer noise stopped and in to the silence came the sound of the two voices we most wanted to hear. They both spoke at the same time.

Dom said, "Shall we put our little pinnies on and join in, Carl?" And Carl said, "And here's one I prepared earlier." He picked up a plate with nothing on it and tilted it gently. His eyes looking straight ahead as though addressing a TV camera, he then gave this brilliant imitation of someone on a television programme all about cookery.

Luce and I were creased up laughing but I noticed that Sarah and Clarissa looked extremely hacked off. When Carl had finished, Luce and I clapped but Sarah sneered and said, "Very funny, ha-ha Carl," and promptly turned her back on him. Dom turned to Luce and me. "I don't think Carl's little sister appreciates his great comic talents."

"Oh, so Sarah is Carl's sister," I said, slowly piecing it all together.

"That's quite unusual," said Luce, voicing my own thoughts, "to have both sisters and both brothers being good friends."

"Well, the girls are friends," Dom said jokingly. "I don't know about us two though!"

Carl winked and said, "No, we're more partners really." Then they both sniggered as though they were having a private joke. Clarissa was not amused.

"Can't you two go and play on the motorway or something, instead of plaguing us all day long?"

"Come on, Carl. Let's go and play darts. Want to come?"

This last question was tossed casually over his shoulder as they went out. Luce and I glanced quickly at each other and it was obvious we were both desperate to say, "Yes, please," but Clarissa and Sarah were back to their cakes so there was nothing we could do really.

"Perhaps when we've finished making the cakes," Luce called out hastily. I hoped it was only me who noticed the keenness in her voice.

The moment the cakes were safely in the oven I dropped a hint about the darts and we all went up to the attic, Sarah and Clarissa very reluctantly. We played two games of 301, then Clarissa and Sarah said they were going down to see if the cakes were ready. Luce and I kept quiet.

The atmosphere after they'd gone was somehow more charged and I could feel Dom's eyes on me. All the talk up till then had been about the game, but Dom suddenly sat down and said, "Are you definitely coming to Finsbury, Jaimini?"

"Er, well, it's not definite. I mean, there's the entrance exam, isn't there? And also it's quite expensive…"

"What about you?" Carl asked Luce.

"No way," Luce answered with a shrug.

"You ought to try," Carl said. "Nobody thought *I'd* get in, but I did."

There was a long pause while Luce took this in, then I watched as her eyes changed.

"Perhaps I ought to try, Jaimes," she breathed in wonder at the new-found possibility.

And then my eyes must have taken on the same rapturous expression because the outlook seemed suddenly not so grim any more. Luce and I looked at each other, eyes dancing. Now we were getting somewhere. If we could *both* go to Finsbury, instead of just me, and Carl and Dom would be there as well, it wouldn't matter quite so much about the Café Club. The others would soon find two more people to fill our places.

For some reason a shadow fell across my excitement when I thought of two other people working at the café instead of us. Don't be silly, I told myself forcefully.

I don't know if Luce had been thinking along the same lines as I had, but she suddenly said, "Tell you what, let's all bike over to the café. It's Leah on duty and the others might be there. We often go there on Saturday afternoons."

"Sounds good," answered Dom lightly. Carl just nodded. We went down to tell Sarah and Clarissa, but they weren't at all keen to go. Sarah just said, "I'm not biking all that way," and Clarissa said, "Me neither." So we left them with their cakes and rode off happily to the café with the only two people we really wanted to be with.

Sure enough, as soon as we walked into the café we spotted Andy, Tash and Fen. The table next to theirs was empty so the four of us sat down. I didn't know about Luce, but I suddenly felt rather embarrassed turning up with two boys. It was almost like having real boyfriends.

I saw Fen and Tash look surprised and even a bit impressed. Andy's eyes, on the other hand, narrowed suspiciously. At least you'd think it was a suspicious look if you didn't know her, but in fact she always does that when something unexpected happens. It's as though she's sizing it up and it's important not to react until she's decided what she really thinks. And that's not an instant thing. It takes time.

I introduced everybody and I must admit I was quite pleased that Dom and Carl seemed genuinely pleased to be meeting our friends. In fact, when Leah came out of the kitchen, Dom immediately asked to be introduced to her as well.

"Hi, Leah," I called quietly. She waved and smiled before turning to her customers. I noticed a look pass between Carl and Dom. I'd seen that look on boy's faces before. They obviously thought Leah was nice-looking. A pang of jealousy pierced right through me, but I told myself very firmly that that was stupid. It was Luce and me that Carl and Dom liked, and that was the end of that.

Andy's look of suspicion turned to something even stronger as time went on. She was taking in every word that everyone said, and for some reason or other I got the impression she didn't like Dom or Carl.

"Right, I'm off," she suddenly said to everyone's surprise. "See ya."

"See ya," we all answered, but after she'd gone the atmosphere seemed to go too and we all gradually broke up.

"Please let him suggest that we meet again," I prayed silently as we headed for the door. My prayer was semi-answered.

"You've got my number," he said. "Give me a ring if you want."

Surely this is the wrong way round, I thought. He should ring *me*, shouldn't he? And there was Carl saying exactly the same thing to Luce.

Life's a funny thing, I reflected as I walked home. For some reason or other I couldn't get rid of the mental image of Luce frantically licking the end of her ball-point so that she could write Carl's number on the back of her hand.

The next day I woke up with a sinking feeling that turned immediately to one of elation at the thought of Dom, then slipped back into neutral as I remembered the events of yesterday.

At breakfast time Mum and Dad both tried to be pleasant and normal. It was perfectly obvious they'd been talking about me and made a decision to be firm and positive about Finsbury Leighton. Me, I just felt confused about it all. Perhaps I would like it there? I couldn't bear it if I wasn't able to see Dom any more, but on the other hand, whatever anyone says, you only stay real friends with the people you go to school with and see every day. And I don't want to lose my friends.

"I know you're dead against the thought of Finsbury Leighton at the moment," Dad began gently, but I interrupted him.

"I'm not *dead* against it."

The quick glance that flew between Mum and Dad spoke a thousand words. I'd thrown them right off balance because they were expecting another big scene from me.

"Well, that's good," said Dad, disarmed, and Mum decided to push me just a little further.

"In that case, perhaps you'd like to come and have a look round the school tomorrow morning?" she suggested.

"Have you already made the appointment?"

"Y-yes."

"OK. Can Luce come?"

"Luce? What, Lucy Edmunson?"

"Yes," I said, a little impatiently.

"But … why?"

"Because she's interested in going there."

Mum and Dad's hopeful faces dropped.

"I don't think Luce would manage the entrance exam," Mum told me gently.

"She's going to work really hard."

"Even so…" Again I didn't miss the look that passed between Mum and Dad. Nobody spoke as we cleared the breakfast dishes. I think that Mum and Dad were afraid that any more words might break that delicate thread of improvement in my attitude. Personally, I only didn't speak because I was thinking. Part of me felt that the whole thing was hopeless and there was probably no way that Luce *would* get into the school, then I'd be stuck there on my own, which would be awful, except for the fact that Dom would be there. But on the other hand, Dom wasn't *that* bothered about seeing me again, or he would have said he'd phone me.

Less than five minutes later the phone rang. Dad answered it and handed it to me. My heart immediately started speeding. Already, I thought. I was wrong. He *does* like me.

"Hello, Jaimini?"

"Yes."

"Can you give me Luce's number, please?"

"Who was that?" Mum asked, trying for her I'm-not-really-that-interested tone of voice.

"A friend of Dominic's, wanting Luce's number." I tried to make my voice light but inside I was beginning to get really knotted up. A few minutes later the phone rang again. This time I grabbed it and went out of the kitchen but it was only Luce. You'd have thought she'd just won the lottery the way she sounded.

"Jaimes, my life has been transformed!" she announced ecstatically. "I am in twenty-third heaven because guess who rang? Oh, you know, don't you? Carl… And guess what? He wants to meet me at the café tomorrow. Has Dom phoned, because we could all go together?"

"No, Dom hasn't phoned and I'm supposed to be having a tour round Finsbury Leighton tomorrow with Mum and Dad. I thought you might like to come, too."

"Well, I would normally, but now Carl's phoned… What time are you going?"

"In the morning."

"Oh, sorry Jaimes, that's when I'm meeting Carl. Oh, I'm so happy I can't tell you. No school for a whole week and Carl tomorrow." She paused and I imagined her expression on the other end of the phone suddenly changing to one of concern. Those eyebrows of hers could knit together like nothing you've ever seen before.

"I'm sorry Dom hasn't phoned yet, Jaimes, but why don't you phone him?"

"I might," I said noncommittally. "Luce, I was talking to Mum and Dad this morning…"

"Oh, that makes a change," joked Luce, still bubbling.

"And they reckoned it's quite difficult to get into Finsbury. You're going to have to work really hard, you know."

There was a pause while Luce weighed this up. "Right Jaimes, let's set to work. You've got to coach me in every subject. I'm determined to pass that test and go to the same school as you and Carl and Dom."

The phone rang twice more that morning. The first time it was Tash. She sounded very flustered and anxious. "We're having a meeting tomorrow at three o'clock at the café," she told me hesitantly. "Can you come? And we were going to ask Luce too?"

"Er … OK, but what's it about, this meeting?"

"I'll, er, tell you tomorrow. See you."

So they were having a meeting, were they? Why did something tell me that the meeting was for my benefit?

The next phone call was from Luce again. "Carl just phoned me again, Jaimes. That's twice in one morning!"

Does she think I can't count or something? I thought rather cruelly. But I softened when I heard her next words. "He phoned me to say that Dom is going to the café tomorrow too, and to make sure *you* were there! Isn't that wonderful?"

"Why didn't Dom phone me himself?" I asked, probably sounding like a spoilt child.

"I dunno," said Luce impatiently. "All I know is that Dom made a special point of telling Carl to phone me back to make sure you would be there."

"But I won't, will I?"

"What!"

"I'm going to look round Finsbury, remember?"

"Oh, no! I didn't think of that." Luce sounded devastated. "Why don't you phone him back and arrange it for later in the day," she said breathlessly.

"Yeah, OK," I agreed wearily, thinking how complicated it was all getting, because I was supposed to be at Tash's great meeting too. "Did Tash phone you?" I asked Luce.

"No…"

"Oh, well, she might. Anyway, we'd better get ready for your first coaching session, hadn't we?"

"Yes, I'll be round at your place in half an hour."

After staring at the phone for about a minute I rang Dom's number.

"Hello."

"Hello, Mrs Bede. Can I speak to Dom, please?"

"Er … y-yes. Who's speaking, please?"

"Jaimini Riva."

There was a tiny pause, then she sounded more friendly.

"Oh, Jaimini, yes dear. I'll just get Dom."

A few seconds later I could hear a great war whoop of delight coming from somewhere in the Bede house. My nervousness was replaced by elation. Dom was obviously pretty happy that I'd phoned. I imagined the little scene at his house.

"Dom. It's Jaimini Riva on the phone."

"Jaimini Riva! YESSSSS!" (punching the air with fist, rushing to the phone in eager antici-pation of hearing the wonderful voice once more).

I was jarred out of my daydream by various clicks in my ear, then his voice came on the line. He *did* sound happy. He *must* like me.

"Hi, Jaimini."

"Hi, Dom. Listen, I'm sorry I can't make tomorrow morning. That's when I'm going round Finsbury Leighton with Mum and Dad, you see…"

"Oh, right…"

I was biting my tongue feeling desperate to say, "but what about tomorrow afternoon?" only I wanted *him* to say it.

"Never mind – another time," he said lightly.

My mind whirled through the possibilities. He couldn't make tomorrow afternoon because he'd got a dentist appointment. He couldn't make it because he was going to meet another girl. No! Horror of horrors! Perhaps he was just being shy? No, that wasn't Dom's style. Maybe he didn't want to appear too keen. Yes, that was it. We were both playing the same game. Neither of us wanted to appear too keen and yet we both were. All this flashed through my mind in about two seconds flat.

"I could make tomorrow afternoon. What about you?" I finally blurted out.

"Er … no … I've got to take my rabbit to the vet's."

"Oh, Dom, I'm really sorry, I didn't know your rabbit was ill. Well, I didn't even know you had a rabbit, actually…" Oh, why did I go bumbling on, sounding so juvenile, when I was nervous? Then I distinctly heard a noise like a stifled laugh on the other end of the phone.

"Dom?"

"Oh, sorry. It's really quite ill, you see."

Oh, poor Dom. He was obviously very attached to his rabbit. That hadn't been a laugh I'd heard. He must have been close to tears.

"What's his or her name?" I asked.

"Beetroot," he replied, "and it's female." Again I heard the catch in his voice as though he could hardly bear to talk about it. I thought I'd better ring off.

"Oh well, good luck at the vet's. I mean, I hope Beetroot gets better soon."

He didn't answer. He must have been really depressed about it all.

"See you soon then," I tried.

"Yeah, see you. Bye."

I put the phone down and stared out of the window, running the conversation back in my head. When I got to the bit about Dom's rabbit, I felt the blood rush to my face. Beetroot! *Beetroot!* What did he take me for, an idiot? You don't have a rabbit and call it Beetroot, do you?

I frowned and recalled Dom's cracking voice. He seemed very moved. Then I thought back to the beginning of the phone call. Mrs Bede's voice. She'd sounded somehow confused or embarrassed, which wasn't at all like Mrs Bede. She'd hesitated, that was it. She wasn't sure who it was who wanted to speak to Dom. Did that mean there was a whole queue of girls or something, and I was just one of them?

I pressed my knuckles into my cheeks to try and make the hot feeling go away. My heart was beating faster. "Please let me be totally wrong about this, God," I prayed, looking at the sky. I was beginning to feel like a really big fool. It looked horribly as though Dom was carrying out the joke of the century on me – telling me all sorts of stupid lies to get out of seeing me again. But why? And why did Carl tell Luce to make sure I'd be in the café because Dom wanted me there?

Chapter 4

On Monday morning I woke up with a very positive plan in my head. In the afternoon I would go to the vet's, which was about half-way between Dom's and my home. I would be extremely discreet but I would keep watch during the whole afternoon, and if Dom didn't appear, then I'd know I'd been tricked. The only trouble with this plan was that if he wasn't there, I'd want to know where he was. If only Andy hadn't seemed so scornful about Dom and Carl, I would have contacted her and asked her advice. She was the spy amongst us all, after all. But there was no way I could contact Andy. It would have been too embarrassing.

At ten o'clock I was standing in the foyer of Finsbury Leighton School with Mum and Dad and the headmistress, Miss Bernard. She pronounced it with the emphasis on the *nard* bit, which immediately made her sound really posh. She shook hands with me and it felt as though I was holding a bit of old rubber or something.

There were loads of huge plaques over the foyer walls, which listed previous head boys and girls as well as all sorts of teams, the teachers and the governors. Why doesn't she get on with the guided tour instead of explaining all these boring plaques? I kept thinking, and eventually she did.

"Of course, the ETmosphere is QUAte different when the pupils are here," smiled Miss Bernard. "It's all so much LAVElier," she added with a little laugh that sounded about as genuine as Dom's phone call. Oh, why do my thoughts always come back to Dom? I asked myself for the hundredth time.

"This is the IT room – that's information technology," she added turning to Mum and

Dad, then she tried unsuccessfully to get friendly with me, by leaning towards me with a little laugh and saying, just loudly enough for Mum and Dad to hear, "Parents these days, get very confused with the educational jargon that is so familiar to you and me, Jaimini."

"My dad works in computers, actually," I told her, which made her face go from perky to droopy in one move. My dad winked at me at that moment and I smiled back because I could tell he appreciated my quick wit.

As we went from room to room I tried to imagine Dom sitting in the class. It wasn't till we came to the end of the tour, that I realized I hadn't really been looking properly at the school or listening to Miss Bernard at all. I'd just been daydreaming about Dom and even imagining myself sitting next to him. That was stupid because he was in the year above me, so of course we wouldn't be in any of the same classes.

"Well, what do you think?" Dad asked me when we were back at the car.

"It's difficult to tell without the pupils being there," I said, honestly. And one pupil in particular, I added to myself. Mum and Dad didn't press me any further. I think they were just happy that at least I wasn't totally against the idea of going to the place.

That afternoon I walked to the vet's and thought on the way about Luce and what a huge change had come over her. The previous afternoon she'd come round to my house and we'd worked together for over two hours. If she didn't understand something she'd get me to go over and over it until she did. I had to admire her. I'd also told her all about my phone call to Dom and she'd put my mind at rest. "Don't worry," she'd said. "You're trying to read too much into a simple little phone call. Just take it at face value and remember that Carl said Dom wanted you to be at the café."

I settled myself a little distance away from the vet's on a wall, with my back against a hedge. I pressed myself into the hedge, which was most uncomfortable but couldn't really be avoided if I was to blend with my surroundings, and took out a magazine.

Keeping watch over the top of the magazine wasn't particularly easy because I had to look in both directions and also look out for anyone coming out of the vet's entrance. I had put my hair in a bun and was wearing a denim hat with a big peak. I sat like this for nearly an hour feeling more and more bored and equally stupid, until finally I decided I couldn't put up with staying there for even a second longer. I was getting some very funny looks from people who had spotted me on their way into the vet's and then again on their way out!

When I arrived at the gates of the Bedes' house, I hesitated. This was going to be very tricky because the drive was so long. I could hardly go crunching up it, then look for a hiding place nearer to the house, but on the other hand I couldn't see the house at all from where I was. In the end I walked about one hundred metres down the road to a public phone box and punched in Dom's number, which naturally I knew by heart. Once again his mother answered. Trying not to let my voice sound shaky, I spoke with a strong Australian accent.

"Could I speak to Dominic, please?"

"Yes, certainly. Who shall I say is calling?"

I'd not thought of a name so I just said the first thing that came into my head. "Raquel."

"All right. Hold the line, please."

Mrs Bede was speaking very clearly as though Australians might not quite be able to understand the English telephone system. A moment later I heard the same clicks as last time I'd phoned, then Dom's voice, sounding just a teeny bit unsure of himself.

"H–hello?"

I put the phone down.

For the next two or three minutes I stayed in the phone box until my heartbeat gradually slowed down. The reason it took a long time was because I was feeling so angry. Dom had really taken me for an idiot. He wasn't at the vet's, so he could easily have met me. I felt like marching up to his front door and demanding an explanation, but when I'd calmed down I realized that there might of course be some very ordinary reason why he hadn't gone to the vet's. Then I had a brilliant idea. I picked up the phone and punched in the same number. Once again Mrs Bede answered.

"Hello."

"Oh, hello Mrs Bede, it's Jaimini Riva. Could I speak to Clarissa, please?"

"Hello, Jaimini, yes of course. I'll just get her."

"Hi, Jaimini," came Clarissa's rather high voice a moment later. No clicks this time I noticed.

"Hi, Clarissa. I just wondered if you wanted to meet me at the café? Dom was going to come but he's had to take his rabbit to the vet's, hasn't he?"

"Rabbit? To the vet's?"

"Yes." (Should I say the name of the rabbit? No better not. I might have misheard it and I didn't want to appear too gullible in Clarissa's eyes.)

"Oh y-yes – his rabbit. Yes, that's right. He

71

did say something about that. I remember now. I don't usually take that much notice of what Dom's doing, but yes, you're right…"

I felt a lovely sense of relief flowing through me. So Dom hadn't been leading me on. He really *did* have a rabbit.

"Actually, the rabbit's much better today, so I don't expect Dom took it to the vet's after all…"

I was feeling happier by the second, but there was just one more question I had to ask. "What's the name of his rabbit? He *did* tell me, but I've forgotten."

There was a long pause, then she said, "Er, it's got a funny name, it's called Be True… I think he named it that when he was little. He's had it for ages, you see."

Be True. Thank goodness I hadn't mentioned the name Beetroot. She would have taken the mickey out of me for ever. I only hoped Dom hadn't thought I'd said Beetroot. I felt my face turning into one at the thought of it.

"I'd love to come to the café, Jaimini, but I

can't because I said I'd help Mum this afternoon, you see."

"Oh, that's OK," I quickly reassured her, as I suddenly remembered I was supposed to be meeting Tash in the café at three o'clock and it was now after three-thirty.

As I hurried to the café I thought over the conversation with Clarissa. She hadn't sounded one hundred per cent convincing, but I wanted to believe her, so I did. Also I kept remembering what Luce had said yesterday, that I shouldn't keep reading things into what people said. I was certainly becoming an expert conversation analyser these days! Once inside the café I rushed over to where Fen and Tash were sitting.

"Hi, sorry I'm late," I said, suddenly feeling self-conscious. The blood rushed to my face so I quickly started talking to hide my embarrassment. "Where are the others?"

"Andy's on duty and Leah's gone out for the day. We thought Luce was with you," Fen said, with a question mark in her voice.

"I think she's with Carl," I said, which made

me feel even more embarrassed, though why it should I didn't really know. Maybe because Fen and Tash seemed so disapproving.

Jan passed our table at that moment and put a hand on my shoulder. "What would you like, pet?" she asked me with her usual smile.

"Lemonade please, Jan."

"Jaimini," Tash began, leaning forwards slightly with her elbows on the table and her shoulders hunched up.

She'd only uttered one word – my name – yet I knew she was about to say something about Dom. I felt myself wanting to spring to his defence whatever Tash said.

Jan put my lemonade down on the table and went off again before Tash spoke. "Andy's got something to tell you," was all she managed, before slumping back in her seat as though even that one little sentence had required a monumental effort. Tash can't bear to upset people, so whatever Andy wanted to say, she must have really believed it needed saying. All the same, by now I was even ready to tell a lie to defend Dom. It's funny, isn't it, how friends getting together behind your back can have that effect on you?

As if on cue Andy appeared at our table, glanced round to check Jan wasn't observing her having a break, then sat down at the table and looked me straight in the eyes as only Andy can. She didn't squirm or look uncomfortable. She didn't look anything except normal.

"I was talking to Jan and Becky earlier on, and they told me that Luce was in here this morning with Carl."

"Yes, I know," I said in a voice that sounded suitably so–tell–me–something–new…

"And apparently Dom was with them, too."

My eyes must have shown my surprise, even though I managed to answer calmly enough, "Yeah, he wanted me to join him actually, but I had to go to look round Finsbury Leighton this morning."

Andy didn't react at all to that. She just carried on talking as though I hadn't spoken. "Apparently, when Luce went to the loo, Carl asked Jan what the name of the girl with the long blonde hair was. He said he thought he might know her. Jan said it was Leah Bryan and then Carl started trying to find out where she lived, but Jan decided he was getting a bit too curious and she wouldn't tell him."

While Andy had been telling me this my mouth had been getting drier and I had started to worry on Luce's behalf. It looked horribly as though Carl was wanting to move on to Leah! But still I didn't want the others to know that their information was making me feel at all insecure.

"Yeah. Dom mentioned to me that he thought he'd seen Leah somewhere around. Obviously Carl has seen her around, too," I lied, smiling at Andy, then at Tash and Fen. Andy didn't smile back. Tash and Fen looked down.

"A bit later," Andy went on, "when Luce was talking to a customer she knew, apparently Dom called Becky, got chatting, then steered the conversation skilfully round to how often we all worked, and seemed particularly interested in me, asking when I'd next be on duty."

My body felt as though it couldn't move properly and my mouth felt drier than a desert, but still I managed to shrug and say, "So?"

"He referred to me as 'that pretty little one with the short dark hair'," Andy finished off. And that did it. I could have cried and yet still I kept trying to defend Dom.

"He's just a curious sort of person that's all…" I didn't sound convincing, even to myself.

"I'll tell you what I think," Andy said, fixing me with her big dark eyes. "I think Dom and Carl are playing some sort of boys' game – trying to score points or something. I'm not exactly sure what, but I *am* sure of one thing … they are *not* to be trusted."

She paused to wait for my reaction. I felt so empty and lost, and yet *still* I couldn't bring myself to believe that Dom didn't really like me at all. Then I slowly realized something…

"Hang on a sec," I said turning to Tash, "it was yesterday when you phoned me to arrange this meeting, and all that Andy has just told me she only found out from Jan and Becky this afternoon!"

Tash looked embarrassed. Andy was about to say something but I cut her off.

"You're just jealous, aren't you!" I practically spat at Andy. "You've made this whole thing up because you want Dom for yourself. I suppose you're trying to fix up Carl and Leah while you're at it. You've even dragged poor Tash into it to make it more convincing. Well, it won't work, Andy. I can't stand jealousy, so why don't you go and get a life – or at least get yourself your *own* boyfriend!"

With that I stomped off, the picture of Andy's huge, hurt eyes still in my head. My heart was pounding when I reached the door. I just had to get out. But my dramatic exit wasn't to be.

Hurtling through the door came Luce, obviously bubbling over with happiness and full of something mind-blowingly interesting to tell me. She didn't notice the anguish on my face, just dragged me to the nearest table, shoved me down in a chair, sat down herself and then launched into the following speech.

"I've been studying like mad. Carl is really pleased we're both going to be at the same school…"

"Yes, but you might not…"

"You've no idea how much more academic I've become. Mum and Dad think I must have a screw loose or something… Anyway, I've discovered this great new drama class on Saturdays. That's what I came here to tell you about… Where are the others?" (looking round) "Oh, there they are… I'll tell them all about it afterwards. You've just got to come to it, Jaimes, it sounds really terrific. Look." (thrusting a well fingered sheet of paper in front of me) "See – drama class – teenagers – Cableden Community Centre – improvisations, sketches, shows. *Shows*, Jaimes! I love shows. I spoke to her on the phone, the teacher, Sally Ahlers she's called, and she sounded really nice. She explained that as long as I go on Wednesday…"

"I thought it was on Saturdays?"

"Yes it is, except for this week, when it's Wednesday."

"That sounds a bit odd."

"Yes, never mind that. Isn't it brilliant? You *will* come along, won't you?"

"Y-yes, I expect so."

"Great! Let's talk to the others about it."

"Er – I've really got to go, Luce."

"That's all right. I'll tell the others and I'll speak to you later."

"OK. Bye."

She was gone like a whirlwind. Before I even made it to the door I saw her sneak up behind Andy, who had got back to work and was carrying a heavily-laden try. Luce covered Andy's eyes while asking in a peculiar deep voice, "Who is it?"

"I expect it's probably Luce," came the reply, "as none of the others would be so idiotic as to cover my eyes when I'm delicately balancing a great load of cups and glasses."

"Oh yes, sorry," Luce apologized, quickly removing her hands.

"That was a pretty silly thing to do," Jan

hissed at Luce as she passed behind her to another table.

"Sorry," Luce mouthed back, then pretended to shoot herself in the head while briskly approaching Fen and Tash's table. Unfortunately, her approach was a bit too brisk and she tripped over Tash's bag and lunged at the table as only Luce can. I saw her thrust the tatty paper with the drama club details down on the table, then I slipped out of the café and started to make my lonely way home. I wasn't lonely for long though.

"Jaimes! Jaimes!" Someone was yelling my name from the distance. I turned round to see Luce staggering along. "Stop! Jaimes, I've been trying to attract your attention for ages."

I waited till she caught up with me, then we walked on together.

"What's up with Andy?"

Uh-oh. I was hoping Luce wouldn't notice, because I didn't want to have to tell her what Andy had said about Carl. It seemed too cruel when Luce and he were obviously getting on really well together.

"What do you mean?"

"Oh, nothing – I just thought she seemed a bit subdued. Come to think of it, so were Fen and Tash."

"What do they think about the drama club?" I asked, to change the subject.

"Andy isn't very keen because she's already got loads of sport and PE things that she does. She said she didn't think Leah would be interested either because of all her music. But Tash and Fen want to come along on Wednesday – and you'll come, won't you, Jaimes?"

"Yes, but what about the café? It's Fen's turn, isn't it?"

At that moment we heard someone calling our names from far behind. We both turned round to see a small figure approaching.

"It's Tash!" Luce said, peering into the distance. Then she clapped her hand to her mouth. "I forgot to pay!"

"Did you have a drink?"

"Oh no, I didn't, did I?"

"But *I* did, and *I* forgot to pay."

"Don't worry, I paid for you," Tash puffed, catching the tail end of our conversation. I hoped and prayed she hadn't come rushing after us to talk about Dom and Carl, because that was the last subject under the sun I felt like discussing. I needn't have worried. Typical Tash, she was acting completely normally, as though my little outburst hadn't even happened.

"Fen's just doing a bit of shopping for her mum, but we were thinking about the drama club. It's Fen's turn to work on Wednesday. She was wondering if you could do her duty, Jaimini?"

"The only trouble is I was going to go to the drama club, too. Can't Leah or Andy do it?"

"No, because their two families are going out together for the day. It's been arranged for ages." Tash shrugged good-naturedly. "Never mind, I don't mind missing it..."

"No, you can't do that, Tash. You want to come too," I said. "But maybe none of us need miss it. I've just had a burst of inspiration. What about Clarissa?"

"Brilliant, Jaimes," cried Luce, then she turned to Tash and said, "Cinderella, you *shall* go to the ball, because Clarissa can work at the café!"

"Do you think Jan will mind?"

"Come to my place, and let's phone Jan at the café just to sound her out about the whole idea," I suggested.

"I've got to get back to look after Peta because Mum and Dad are going out," Tash said, looking at her watch. "I'll phone from there and let you know."

So we parted ways and I let Luce burble on to her heart's content about the wonderful Carl all the way to my house, because I didn't want to put doubts in her mind. I knew how awful that felt.

The phone was ringing as we went in.

"Hi, it's Tash. Everything's arranged. Jan wasn't particularly chuffed at the idea of Clarissa working in the café, but she said that just this once she'd allow it as long as Clarissa could get a bit of practice tomorrow."

"Great!" I said, while Luce tugged at my

sleeve and said, "Can she do it?" in a hoarse sort of whisper.

"Now we just need to ask Clarissa herself," Tash pointed out.

"Let's go now," I suggested.

"The only trouble is Peta."

"Bring her with us. It won't matter. We'll come over to you. See you soon."

I filled Luce in and we went straight off to Tash's. We all loved going to Tash's house because her little sister Peta is only just three and she's extremely lively and entertaining. She comes out with amazingly amusing things and she's really cute.

Chapter 5

"Some peoples comin'," came Peta's loud, excited voice from somewhere within the house as we rang the bell. The door opened about fifteen centimetres, then stopped because it banged into something. Peta's little grinning face appeared very high up in the crack, so we assumed she must have been standing on a chair, then the door slammed shut again as we heard her yell out, "It's Loosey Goosey and Janey Bootiful."

She's always called us by these names. Mine is the only one of the six names that she doesn't turn into a rhyme. It's very flattering to be called "beautiful" or rather "bootiful", and Peta has never been able to manage Jaimini, so she says Janey instead, which I really like.

"Have you let them in?" came Tash's voice from upstairs.

"No, I shut the door again," Peta answered.

"Well, let them in, silly thing," Tash called back.

"OK."

We stood on the doorstep wondering what would happen next and not minding at all about having to wait. A moment later exactly the same thing happened again – the fifteen centimetre gap, and the little high up face peering through it.

"'Sgot stuck," announced Peta while she contorted all her features in a big effort to open the door, which couldn't possibly open any further because the chair was in the way.

"Get down from the chair and move it, Peta," I told her firmly.

Peta didn't say anything, just solemnly clambered down from the chair, but she must have pressed against the door while she was doing it, because once again it shut in our faces.

We collapsed in giggles and waited to see what would happen next. I suggested we went round to the back door, but Luce said she didn't want to miss the fun, so we stayed on the front doorstep. After another few seconds, the door opened for the third time and the little face with the big eyes appeared at the fifteen centimetre crack.

"Silly ole Peta shut ve door," we were told, which made us smile.

"Right, get down from the chair but *don't* touch the door this time," I instructed Peta. In answer she regarded me gravely and said, "I clean my teeth two times, you know."

"Do you?" I humoured her.

"Yes."

"Well, are you going to open the door?"

"Yes."

"Go on, then."

"Janey?"

"Yes?"

"How many times do you clean your teeth?"

"Same as you. Once at night. Once in the morning."

"Vats not ve same as me."

"When do you clean your teeth, then?"

"One time in ve morning and ve uvver time at bed time."

"Well, that's the same as me then."

"No, cos you was one time at night and one time in ve morning and I was one time in ve morning and one time…" She suddenly tailed off and looked at Luce as though she was finding me too boring for words. "Are you coming to Calissas too, Loosey Goosey?"

"Yes I am, so you'd better let us in, hadn't you?"

Tash's voice yelled out again, "Have you let them in, Peta?"

"Stop shouting. We're talking!" Peta tossed crossly over her shoulder, then turned back to us with an enormous beam as though she'd really enjoyed telling her big sister off. We were about to repeat the instructions about moving the chair when the door was flung open by a very exasperated-looking Tash, who had tucked Peta up under one arm and moved the chair away with the other.

"Little sisters have got to be the very worst things in the entire world," Tash commented. "In fact, if I had to choose between a little sister and a pet slug, I think I'd probably go for the slug!" she went on, warming to her theme.

"And you could call the sweet little slug Peta!" Peta finished off triumphantly.

Tash looked even more exasperated then, because Peta hadn't even clicked that her big sister was trying to be cross with her. Of course I knew Tash was only joking, but in a way it made me feel sad because Mum has been trying to get pregnant for years, ever since I was two in fact, and I'd absolutely love to have a little sister or brother.

"Right, let's get going," Luce said. "Clarissa, here we come!" she added.

"Listen 'ere you crumb!" Peta shouted cheerfully.

"I didn't say that," Luce protested. "I said, Clarissa here we come." This second time Luce spoke very slowly and clearly, but Tash and I faced the other way so Peta wouldn't see our amusement, otherwise she'd only keep repeating it to get more and more laughs out of us.

We put Peta in her buggy but had great difficulty doing up the straps because she kept struggling to get out. "I want to see Fenny Penny," she cried.

"No, Fen's not here yet," Tash said, looking at her watch.

"Yes, I am," said a familiar voice, and we all turned round to see Fen standing there.

"Going to see Larissa Crumb," Peta informed her excitedly.

"Are we? Let's go then," Fen replied, and as we all set off on the great expedition the rest of us filled Fen in on what we'd arranged.

"Hang on a sec," said Fen, after about twenty minutes. "Has anyone actually phoned Clarissa? I mean, what if she's not in?"

We all looked rather ashamed of ourselves. What a stupid mistake to have made. "Oh well, it's too late now," Tash said. "Let's just start praying."

"Fank you for ve world so sweet," Peta's voice rang out, to the amusement of a couple walking past us at that moment.

"Not that sort of praying, Peta," Tash told her little sister. Then for our benefit, "She's been going to nursery school. She's obviously picked it up from there."

"Fank you for ve food we eat.

Fank you for ve birds what sing,

Fank you golf ball evryfink."

"Not golf ball, God," Tash corrected her.

"God," repeated Peta dutifully, then she spent the rest of the journey making up her own little song. The tune was a mixture of very high and excruciatingly high notes, and the lyrics consisted of just one word – "God!"

"Do you think we'd better shut her up?" Luce said to Tash as we approached the Bede's home. "I mean, we don't want Mrs Bede to think we're Jehovah's Witnesses or something!"

"*Ssh* now, Peta," said Tash, quite sternly. "You've got to be very quiet because we're going inside this big house."

We crunched up the drive and only stopped

once for Peta to whisper something. Crouching down to her level we all waited to hear what she was going to say. It was obviously important because her eyes were filled with awe. "Is it God's house, Tasher Basher?"

"No, it's Clarissa's house, and stop calling me Tasher Basher. I don't like it."

We had arrived at the door by then and Fen knocked firmly just as Peta was solemnly asking us, "Do you think Larissa will mind if I say Larissa Kisser?" So of course we were all in hysterics when Mrs Bede opened the door. Her face was a picture of surprise and irritation at our bad manners until her eyes travelled down and she saw Peta.

"Sorry, Mrs Bede," I began, "just to turn up out of the blue like this, but we were out for a walk with Tash's little sister…"

"Called Peta," interrupted Peta in such a tiny voice that Mrs Bede had to bend down to hear her.

"Called what, dear?"

"Called Peta, only I'm a girl," Peta explained, very sensibly.

Mrs Bede smiled.

"Well, I don't think that Dom's here actually," she told me, straightening up and seeming very embarrassed.

"Oh, that's all right," I said, with great relief. "It was actually Clarissa we popped in to see."

"Oh, lovely!" Mrs Bede cried, clapping her hands together. It was obviously just as big a relief to her as it was to me. "Come in, come in. Oh my goodness, what a lot of you! Never mind, luckily our house is big enough."

She's positively rambling now, I thought, and the rolled eyes from Luce showed that she had noticed too.

"Clarissa," called Mrs Bede, in an operatic warble.

"Clarissa," yelled Peta, in an extremely accurate imitation which normally we would have cracked up over, but we thought it might seem rather rude, so we sort of giggled nervously for about two seconds.

"I see!" said Mrs Bede, turning to Peta with smiling eyes and dropping to a crouched position in front of her. "So we've got a little parrot here, have we? Hm?"

"Don't you even know if you've got a parrot or not?" Peta asked, in a tone of voice that suggested she thought Mrs Bede must be thick or something.

"Oh no, dear, *we* haven't got a parrot."

"Well, have you got a cat then?" asked Peta sounding quite sorry for Mrs Bede because she didn't have a parrot.

"Yes, we have two cats, a ginger and a tabby," came the reply.

"And have you got a rabbit?" Peta wanted to know.

Oh, you clever little girl, Peta, I thought. You've just asked the very question I wanted to ask.

"A rabbit?"

"Hello, you lot!" Clarissa called out, leaning over the banister at the top of the stairs. So the six million dollar question never did get an answer. I sighed. "Come on up. I've been doing homework and it's a lovely relief to be able to stop for a bit."

We left the buggy in the hall and Tash and Fen half walked, half jumped Peta up the wide staircase.

After a few minutes of general conversation, I judged it to be about the right moment to ask Clarissa our big favour. "Clarissa, we were wondering, would you be interested in earning some money on Wednesday afternoon?"

"No, not really – you see I've got plenty..." Clarissa stopped mid-sentence and shut her mouth firmly, then blushed.

"Do you get lots of money then, lucky thing?" Luce asked in a friendly enough way.

"No but..." Again Clarissa stopped. This time even Luce seemed reluctant to press her any further. I think we were all a bit out of our depth. None of us had ever come across a thirteen-year-old who didn't desperately need more money the entire time!

"What were you going to say, anyway?" Clarissa asked quickly.

Luce explained about the drama club and the café and the rest of us chipped in from time to time.

"Yeah. No problem. I don't mind doing that for you," Clarissa said at the end. "You'll have to show me what to do though, and I'll probably be absolutely hopeless because I'm terribly clumsy, you know."

I could have hugged her. She was being really kind and honest, and of course we were all over the moon that we were going to be able to go to the drama club.

"I'm sure you'll be brilliant at it," Fen said. "Why don't you come along tomorrow afternoon and have a bit of a try out? Who's on duty?"

"It's me," Tash replied.

"OK. That would be good," Clarissa agreed, but she didn't seem to be concentrating. "Where's your little sister?" she asked, looking round.

Tash's head swung from side to side like in one of those shampoo adverts, as she frantically looked round the room for Peta.

"Search party!" screeched Luce. "I'll go outside and check the garden."

"I'll come with you," said Clarissa. "There are lots of little sheds and things."

"You haven't got a pond, have you?" Tash asked, turning pale.

"Yes, we have," Clarissa answered, with the same horror in her eyes as the rest of us had. So we all belted downstairs and out into the garden. For at least five minutes we searched every inch of the garden and every corner of every shed and the garage. Tash borrowed Mr Bede's high boots and waded into the pond looking close to tears. When she was almost in the middle we heard a faint knocking noise.

"Ssh, listen! What's that?" Fen said, and we all stood like statues. The knocking noise was coming from the house. Someone was tapping on one of the windows. We quickly scanned every window and then one by one our rigid bodies melted into relief at the sight of Peta's smiling face and waving hand at one of the first floor windows.

"That's Dom's bedroom," Clarissa told us as Tash waded out of the pond, climbed out of the big boots and legged it with the rest of us to the house, upstairs to Dom's room.

This is going to be interesting, I thought. A part of me hoped I might find a half written letter to "my darling Jaimini", but the other part hoped that I might find the walls plastered with pictures of dozens of girl-friends, then I could be really mad and also have the satisfaction of having found him out.

As it happened there was nothing interesting at all in Dom's bedroom, except for little Peta standing on his bed with her arms clasped firmly round an enormous ginger cat that hung down to her toes and looked extremely uncomfortable, poor thing.

"You little monkey!" Tash said, releasing the cat from Peta's firm grip and hugging her little sister fiercely. "You mustn't ever run off without telling me. I thought … I thought you might have got lost."

"I didn't run, I walked," Peta assured Tash gravely, and we all laughed from the pure relief of having found her all in one piece.

*　　*　　*

The following afternoon we met as arranged at the café, so that Clarissa could meet Jan and get to know the ropes a bit. Tash had phoned me in the morning to say she couldn't be at the café till later when her mum got back, because she had to look after Peta again. So I had agreed to cover the first part of the shift with Clarissa helping me. Luce had gone to Carl's place. She really was smitten. I just kept hoping she wouldn't get hurt.

Funnily enough, Clarissa *was* quite clumsy. I had thought she was only joking when she'd first said that, but once or twice she tripped up or bashed into something. Nothing serious so I didn't worry about it. I wasn't concentrating very hard that day because I kept wondering whether or not to tackle Clarissa about Dom. I played hundreds of opening lines through my mind to see what they sounded like, *"Clarissa, you don't really expect me to believe that Dom's got a rabbit called Be True, do you?"* or, *"Clarissa, may I have a word with you? I really would be grateful if you'd let me know whether Dom really likes me…"* or,

"Clarissa, I can't work Dom out. Can you throw any light on the subject for me?"

In the end I abandoned them all because each one sounded more ridiculous than the last, and it wasn't fair to involve Clarissa. She was doing enough for us by helping out at the café.

A bit later Tash turned up and Clarissa went.

"See you tomorrow," Jan called, cheerfully. "And well done! You've picked up a lot in a short time. I think you'll be a useful reserve if ever this lot find themselves going to the same event again."

Clarissa smiled back, looking grateful and pleased. Tash put on the apron I'd just taken off and started washing up.

"I've got something to tell you," she whispered to me before casting a worried glance in Jan's direction. I realized immediately that this was going to be bad news.

"I'll dry for you, Tash," I said clearly – for Jan's benefit – so she wouldn't wonder why I was still hanging around in the kitchen.

Jan went out almost immediately and I waited for Tash to speak. Kevin was singing as he worked and didn't seem to be taking any notice of us, but all the same Tash spoke very softly because we all know he's got the biggest flappers in England.

"Something fell out of Peta's dungarees yesterday."

I didn't know what Tash was on about at first. At least I couldn't work out the connection between Peta's dungarees and me.

"Look Jaimes, the last thing I want to do is to upset you…"

I just kept drying dishes and feeling sick.

"And Andy's the same…"

"All that stuff that Andy was saying was nothing," I said, because I didn't want her to know how vulnerable I was feeling.

"Well, see if you think the same about this." She cast a surreptitious glance in Kevin's direction as she wiped her hands on a towel, then she took something out of her bag and handed it to me. It was a cassette, a blank one. The way she was handling it I half wondered if it had drugs stashed in it or something.

"It fell out of Peta's dungarees. I played it out of curiosity and realized straight away that she must have picked it up from Dom's room."

"How did you know?"

"Look, Jaimini, take it home and you'll see for yourself."

She had gone back to her washing-up, but I didn't feel like drying any more, so I said goodbye to Jan and Tash. "Ring me later if you want," Tash said as I was going out of the door. I nodded and went home.

Once safely in my bedroom I put the cassette in the tape recorder and this is what I heard. First a loud voice, then a soft one, and so on.

"Hi, Jaimini."

"Hi, Dom. Listen, I'm sorry I can't make tomorrow morning. That's when I'm going round Finsbury Leighton with Mum and Dad, you see…"

"Oh, right… Never mind – another time."

Pause.

"I could make tomorrow afternoon. What about you?"

"Er ... no ... I've got to take my rabbit to the vet's."

"Oh, Dom, I'm really sorry. I didn't know your rabbit was ill. Well, I didn't even know..."

At that point I savagely pressed the STOP button to switch the tape recorder off, and stared fiercely into space.

What was Dom playing at? Why did he record our phone conversation? Did he just happen to have his tape recorder on at the time I phoned? Surely that would have been too much of a coincidence. Was he keeping the recording as a souvenir of me? Maybe the rest of the recording would hold some sort of clue. I pressed PLAY.

"...you had a rabbit, actually."

A very indistinct noise followed my words. I pressed REWIND to listen to it again, but it was no good, I couldn't make it out properly on the tape, so I listened to the next bit of conversation.

"Dom?"

"Oh, sorry. It's really quite ill, you see."

"What's his or her name?"

"Beetroot ... and it's female."

Then there was another indistinct noise.

"Oh well, good luck at the vet's. I mean, I hope Beetroot gets better soon."

There followed such a long pause that I nearly pressed STOP, but then my voice came over softly but clearly.

"See you soon, then."

"Yeah, see you. Bye."

I heard the noise of the receiver being replaced, then the click of the tape recorder being switched off. Then immediately there was another click followed by this.

"H-Hello?"

Click.

So he recorded *all* his phone calls, did he? That meant I could immediately forget the possibility that he was recording my voice to have a memory of me when I wasn't there. On a burst of inspiration I pressed rewind to listen to the very beginning of the tape.

Click.

"Hi, Dom. It's me."

"Oh, hi."

"Do you want to meet me at the bus stop?"

"Er ... what time?"

"Any time you like."

"It's a bit difficult tonight."

Pause.

"Why? You're not going out with someone else, are you?"

Pause.

"You are, aren't you?"

Pause.

"I hate you, Dominic Bede. What's her name, anyway?"

"Jaimini. You don't know her."

"Oh, don't I? Well, I soon will so you'd better watch out. Anyway, I'm glad I'm shot of you if you can drop people just like that. GoodBYE!"

Pause. Click. Gap. Then straight into *my* conversation.

Chapter 6

I was left feeling completely bewildered. I couldn't think of any reason why Dom should be taping our conversations, unless it was just for fun. I had to admit I was cheered up by the conversation with the girl who wanted to meet him at the bus stop, whoever she was. He'd obviously dumped her for me. So why was Tash acting so dramatically about it? She and Andy were really getting into a stew about nothing. All the same I shouldn't have shouted at Andy. I felt guilty about that.

My thoughts were interrupted by a light knock at my bedroom door, followed by Mum coming in.

"Oh, there you are. What are you doing?"

"Oh, just homework."

"Good, because you've got a big day coming up on Thursday, haven't you?"

Mum was nervous, I could tell. She was probably afraid I was about to throw another tantrum about not wanting to go to Finsbury. She looked relieved when I just said, "I wouldn't call it a big day, but I know what you mean."

"So you're happier about going there now?" she asked tentatively.

"I don't know how I feel," I told her honestly.

"Well, that's understandable. Sometimes it's best to let someone else make the decision for you, and that's what parents are for," she said with a smile that I didn't have the energy to return.

With that she left me and my mixed-up thoughts. It was only the phone ringing a few minutes later that snapped me out of my reverie.

"Hi, Jaimes, can I come over?"

It was Luce, sounding not quite her usual self.

"Yes, course you can. See you soon." She was with me in under ten minutes.

"What's up?" I asked her, getting straight to the point.

In answer, she did a huge dramatic sigh and said, "Maybe nothing."

"Well, that tells me a lot!" I joked. "Is it something to do with Carl?"

She nodded. "We went to the Terraced Gardens this afternoon, then he suggested we went to the café. When we got there we sat on our own table, but I couldn't help noticing that Carl's eyes kept straying over to Leah at the other table. He told me he thought he knew her from somewhere but couldn't think where, so I called her over. Well, it was immediately obvious to me that Leah didn't know him from Adam. I know it's stupid to be jealous over such a little thing but I couldn't help feeling uneasy…"

"Have you talked to Leah or any of the others about it?" I asked, carefully.

"No… I could tell Leah wasn't interested in Carl because she went back to her own table at the first opportunity, but it just gave me a horrible feeling."

"Luce…" I said finally.

"What?"

So I told her the whole story of Dom. The rabbit, the cassette, the lot. She listened wide-eyed, drawing her breath in sharply every so often. I also told her what Andy had said about Carl asking after Leah the other day, and what she'd said about Dom asking after Andy herself, *and* about Andy's theory that both of them were involved in some sort of stupid boys' game.

Luce stayed silent when I'd finished speaking, which was certainly unusual for Luce. When she eventually spoke I was quite surprised.

"In everything you've told me, there's actually nothing at all to incriminate Carl or Dom, is there? I mean, Carl still acts as though he really likes me and maybe he genuinely thought he *had* seen Leah somewhere before.

As for Dom, I think Andy's making it all up!"

"What!"

"And I'll tell you why. Because she wants to stop you from going to Finsbury Leighton. She's clever, Andy is. I bet Fen's really worried about the Café Club. I bet she's thinking, 'Oh dear, if Jaimini goes, Jan might not let the rest of us carry on.' I mean, you know how fond Jan is of you. So Fen got Andy to have a go at you."

"But would I definitely have to give up the Café Club if I did get to Finsbury?"

"I'm not sure, but I can understand the others worrying about it all the same."

I frowned.

"Anyway, that's not your problem. Your problem is Dom. And it's all perfectly simple. If he contacts you again, you'll know we were right all along, and if he doesn't, you'll know he's not interested any more."

Sometimes Luce has a surprising way of summing everything up neatly and sensibly.

"Right, let's get down to work," she went on, brightly.

So we worked away for about two hours, during which I thought to myself at least twenty times, am I doing the right thing, encouraging Luce, if she hasn't got much chance of getting into Finsbury anyway?

The following day I woke up with mixed feelings. I felt happy about the drama club, but depressed because I'd got precisely one day before the dreaded entrance exam to Finsbury. Luce had persuaded her parents to put her name down for it, so we were going together.

"Why so thoughtful?" Mum asked me at breakfast time.

"Because I'm worried about Finsbury. If Luce doesn't get in I'll be miserable being there on my own."

"You won't be on your own. You'll have Clarissa … and Dom." She looked at me over the rim of her teacup. How embarrassing. I shrugged as though Dom meant nothing to me, then the phone rang, and I reached for it lazily and said, "Hello," in a very flat voice.

"Hi, Jaimini, it's Dom."

"Dom!" I shot out of my chair, much to Mum's amusement, and raced upstairs with the phone. My brain was doing backflips because it was so lovely to hear his voice again. I'd given up hope and now in one ring of the phone the whole world seemed sunny. "Be sensible, be sensible," a little voice kept reminding me.

"I was wondering if you wanted to go and see *Carnaby Island* with me. It's on at the Odeon."

"When?"

"Well, tonight actually."

"Tonight. Yes, I think so, I'll just check with Mum."

"Oh, sorry Jaimini, there's someone at the door. Can you phone me back when you've asked your mum?"

"Yeah, sure. Bye."

I skipped down the stairs, bouncing with revived spirits, rushed into the kitchen and said, "That was Dominic Bede. He wants to know if I can go to the Odeon tonight with him to see *Carnaby Island*."

I saw the hesitation in Mum's eyes and knew exactly what she was thinking. She was weighing up whether it would be better to say no, as I really shouldn't have a late night the night before my entrance exam, or whether to say yes because the more I saw of Dom the more positive I would feel about Finsbury.

"I don't see why not," she said, with a smile. I ran up the stairs two at a time, waited till my breathing was back to normal, then dialled Dom's number. He answered straight away and I didn't hear any clicks.

"Hi, it's Jaimini. Mum says that's fine."

"Great! I'll meet you there at seven."

"See you later, then."

"Yeah, bye."

I put the phone down and hugged myself. This was a proper date. I felt about seventeen. Just wait till Andy got to hear about this! She'd soon eat her words.

Luce came round a little later to do some more work. She was almost as delighted as I was when I told her Dom had phoned.

"Of course I always knew he would," she said confidently.

We worked for ages and I had to admit Luce was doing really well. She was in with a good chance of passing the exam, even though her teacher was rather dreamy that morning.

We all met together for the drama class outside the Community Centre and compared notes on how we were feeling. Tash and Fen were really looking forward to it, though Fen, typically, was feeling anxious in case anything went wrong while Clarissa was working at the café. Poor Fen always bears the brunt of the responsibility where the Café Club is concerned.

"How do you feel, Jaimes?" Fen asked me.

"She feels a million dollars," Luce answered for me. "Guess who's just phoned her up and invited her to the cinema tonight?"

I watched Tash's expression turn from shock to pleasure. Typical Tash. She still wanted the best for me – even if it meant she was proved wrong along the way. "That's great," she said, sincerely.

"I thought I heard voices," someone said. It was the drama teacher, Sally Ahlers, and she looked really nice.

Her hair was brown and shoulder-length and she had a wide smile and a pretty face. She was dressed extremely trendily. Actually, it's not easy to describe what she was wearing because it was quite a mixture. I'll try. Dark green leggings which may have been thick footless tights, a green, brown and orange sort of enormous tunic, or it could have been a scarf, draped round her over a long floppy-sleeved sort of shirt which was very tight with no buttons. She wore no jewellery or make-up, but had an orange and red scarf tied in a big band on top of her head. Her feet were bare. Her fingernails were bright green and I guessed she was about twenty-eight. The overall impression was brilliant!

"Guess what Luce'll be wearing next time we see her," Tash whispered in my ear.

"Exactly what I was just thinking!" I replied.

"Come on in, girls. Four of you! That's excellent. You haven't got any boys in your wake, have you?" She looked behind each one of us jokingly. "Hm. Pity. I desperately need more boys."

Luce and I gave each other significant looks. Perhaps we could get Dom and Carl to come along.

As we followed Sally in I got the impression of a lot of buzz. There were about twelve people there already – all talking in groups. I recognized some older girls and two older boys from Cableden. There were also two boys and two girls I didn't recognize. The girls looked the same age as us. I felt as though they were watching us. I glanced over once or twice and each time I met the eyes of one of the girls, who looked very striking with golden-blonde permed hair and a tanned face. The moment she saw I was looking she quickly looked away.

Sally set to work immediately. "We're going to have a shot at putting on a potted version of *Grease* for our next show in about twelve weeks time, so I want to do a bit of singing, dancing *and* acting today, so that by the end of the class I can decide exactly who is going to take which parts."

Luce's eyes sparkled as she glanced round at us all. Fen and Tash looked pretty excited, too. I just thought, "What's the betting I'll be chosen to play a boy's part with my hair scraped back, because I'm tall."

"We've only got four boys in the class so please try to persuade some more boys to join," Sally urged us.

"Another four boys from our class at school said they might come," a girl called Alex said.

Then everybody turned to the window because we all heard a noise. It was as though someone had thrown a clod of earth at the wall. The bump was followed by a snigger – a boy's snigger.

"Aha!" said Sally. "It could be that my wish has been granted!" With that she flung open the window and said, "Right, let's have you two in the class. Don't be shy."

How embarrassing for them to be shown up

like that! All eyes were on the door ready to watch the discomfort of the boys who had been spying on the class. Sally Ahlers was no fool.

In through the door came two extremely sheepish-looking boys who were trying to look cool. The brown-faced blonde-haired girl who'd been looking at me obviously knew them and seemed quite pleased to see them.

"Join in, you two," Sally commanded. "We're doing *Grease*. You might find you like it. If you don't, there's no obligation to come back next time." She then proceeded to make the class the fastest moving, most brilliant fun class I've ever been to and by the end of it we were all exhausted, but pleased with ourselves.

"OK, let's sort out the main parts," Sally said as we sat down. "There's a lot of talent here and it's not going to be easy for me to decide who should take which parts." Sally then went through most of the class allocating the slightly lesser parts first. As I had guessed, I was given a boy's part, and so was Tash. Neither of us minded. Fen got the part of Frenchie. She whispered to us that she really wanted to be Riz, which was the second main part, but she didn't mind too much because at least Frenchie was a good part.

Finally, there were only Luce and the girl with the permed hair who hadn't been given a part, and there were only two parts left – the main one, Sandy, and the part of Riz.

"I hope I get Sandy," Luce whispered to me.

"I want to be Sandy," piped up the other girl, whose name was Emma Ludgate. Every time I heard her talk I thought I recognized her voice but I couldn't think where I'd heard it before. I didn't like her. She was so sure of herself, and just assumed she'd be given the role of Sandy because she'd said she wanted it. She threw a supercilious glance at Luce, which had the effect of making Luce sit up straighter.

"We've got a few minutes left. Let's go through Sandy's song, 'You're the one that I want'. Emma, you go first and don't forget the dance movements. I'd like Robert to be Danny." Robert was one of the Cableden older boys. He was an excellent actor *and* singer. Everyone knew he'd get the main boy's part.

Emma sang really well but wasn't very good at the movements. She was flinging herself about too much. It just looked show-offy. She couldn't stop casting glances at Luce and me. I don't think I've ever come across anyone quite so fond of herself as Emma Ludgate. On the other hand, I knew Sally was looking for someone with a lot of confidence and no inhibitions, and there was no doubt about it, Emma's voice was excellent.

Then it was Luce's turn. Luce has got a good voice too, but her acting is her strongest talent. I knew she was nervous, but I also knew she was determined. She began to sing the number with Robert and I felt so proud of her. I realized immediately that all Emma's over-the-top actions were to cover up her self-consciousness, because to play the part of Sandy she was having to pretend she fancied another boy. Luce simply became Sandy. You forgot it was Luce after the first couple of bars. She looked Robert right in the eye and Robert looked right back.

At the end we all clapped like mad, including Sally, who looked really moved by their performance. Of course, she had to be diplomatic for Emma's sake, so she said, "Well, that was really great acting and singing from both of you but I think Lucy seems a little more comfortable in that role, whereas you, Emma, will make an absolutely perfect Riz." Again, we all clapped as Luce sat down beside me looking positively ecstatic. "Well done," the three of us whispered. I couldn't resist sneaking a glance at Emma. She looked daggers back at me as though *I* were the one who'd stolen the main part from her.

"Right," said Sally, dishing out song sheets for us all to take home and learn, "see you next Wednesday."

Luce and I looked at each other in alarm. "Wednesday!" we both mouthed. "I could have sworn she said Saturday," Luce added, looking miffed.

"We can't do Wednesdays," said one of the

boys who had been hauled in by Sally. "We go to Finsbury Leighton, you see, and you have to stay till at least five o'clock."

"Oh, that's a shame," Sally said, while Luce and I looked at each other in horror. Neither of us had any idea that if we went to Finsbury we would *have* to stay at school till five o'clock each day. My mind was doing somersaults trying to work out very quickly what we should do.

Luce turned her worried eyes on me and said urgently, "Think of something, Jaimes," as though I could find the perfect solution with a click of my fingers.

To tell the truth, I wasn't concentrating properly on what Luce was saying because I'd overheard a whispered remark made by one of the Finsbury boys. I couldn't be sure of exactly what he said but it was something about only being there to beat Dom and Carl. I frowned and wondered what he meant by that. I don't think any of the others heard it, because Fen and Tash were looking anxious.

"What about the Café Club?" Luce hissed

at me. And then I understood the worry on Fen's and Tash's faces.

"What am I going to do?" Luce demanded in a helpless whisper, but the other boy was talking.

"Emma won't be able to come either, will you, Emma?" This time Sally looked really worried.

"Is that true, Emma?"

"I might," Emma mumbled, looking rather embarrassed.

"She goes to Finsbury too, you see," the first boy explained.

"What on earth did you go for the main part for, Emma?" Sally asked her, unable to conceal the irritation she was obviously feeling. "You were here when we decided that the regular weekly time was going to be Wednesdays. You must have known you wouldn't be able to do it."

"I thought I might be able to get out of school early," Emma said, but it was clear from the boys' derisive sneers that there was no chance of her doing that.

Wherever had I heard her voice before? And why on earth was Emma so desperate for the main part when she knew she had no chance of coming to the class? I studied her defiant face, and then it came to me. Emma didn't really care about drama at all. She only wanted the main part because she had to be the number one person in every situation. I knew then where I'd heard her voice before. On Dom's tape.

"What's her name, anyway?"

"Jaimini. You don't know her."

"Oh, don't I? Well, I soon will so you'd better watch out."

The four of us set off for the café. Tash and I were going through every boy in our year, considering each one's suitability for joining the class. We'd come up with six, which was good, because although we'd both enjoyed the class, neither of us was particularly bothered about joining on a regular basis. Anyway, it would have been impossible for more than two of us to go to drama regularly, because of the café.

"I was so sure Sally had said the classes were going to be on Saturdays from now on," Luce said for at least the fifth time.

"Look Luce, the fact remains they're going to be on Wednesdays, which means you've got a big decision to make. Are you going to try for Finsbury and give up the drama classes as well as the part of Sandy, or are you going to give up the idea of Finsbury?"

"Which means giving up Carl?" Luce finished off.

"I didn't say that."

"Yes, but that's what giving up Finsbury means, isn't it?"

"Not necessarily."

"Oh, I don't know, Jaimini. What do you think I should do?"

"Well, if *I'm* going to Finsbury, I want *you* to be there, but I couldn't possibly expect you to give up the drama, so I don't know."

We were stuck. It was like getting out of a maze. Whichever route we tried we came to a dead end.

"We don't have to decide right now, do

we?" Luce said finally.

"No," I admitted, "but we haven't got long."

We left it at that and walked the rest of the way to the café in thoughtful silence.

Clarissa was washing up when we went into the kitchen through the back door. She looked hot and tired. Kevin had already gone home and Jan was just coming through to the kitchen from the café.

"Hello, here comes the local amateur dramatic society," Jan said jokingly, and we all laughed, mainly because it was such a relief to see that she was in a good mood. It proved that Clarissa had obviously coped well and no disasters had occurred.

So why was Clarissa looking so worried? Perhaps she'd just found it a strain.

"I'm glad you're here, girls," Jan was saying, "because I'd like to leave very punctually as I'm going out tonight. I wouldn't have left Clarissa to do the lock up, of course, so can I leave you in charge, Fen?"

"Yes, that's fine," Fen answered.

"Oh, no! I've forgotten to transfer the fifty pounds for tomorrow's float to the safe," said Jan, sounding vexed with herself.

"Don't worry, I'll do it," I immediately offered, because I'd been dying to open the safe with the secret code numbers and put in the money that we needed to start the next day. Jan told me the code, and I knew I'd easily remember it, because it was the café's phone number in reverse with a nought instead of the last number.

"How was the class?" Jan went on.

"Fantastic," Fen answered. "Guess who's got the main part of Sandy in the *Grease* show we're going to put on?"

Jan's eyes travelled over us all slowly. "Would it be Miss Lucy Edmunson by any chance?" she asked, with a knowing twinkle.

Luce managed a smile and a nod, but I think Jan must have been surprised by the low key response. Luce's normal reaction would have been to punch the air and screech, *"Yeessss!"*

"Right, I'm off. See you tomorrow."

"Yes, bye," we all called, then turned to Clarissa.

"Was it all right?" Fen asked her.

"Y-yes … fine," Clarissa replied. "Actually, I'd better get going too."

We all dug into our pockets and pulled out various coins which we pooled and gave to Clarissa for her pay.

"Oh, that's all right. I don't need paying, honestly."

"Of course you do. You saved our lives," Tash smiled.

"No, it's all right, really."

"You didn't have any problems, did you?" Fen asked astutely.

"Well … only … one." Clarissa looked down. "One big one," she added softly.

"What? Tell me!" Fen demanded urgently.

For answer Clarissa walked over to the tall cupboard freezer where Kevin always puts his wonderful gateaux. She opened the door and a horrible smell hit us.

"Ugh! Vinegar!" Luce said, holding her nose and backing away.

"Exactly," Clarissa agreed, looking very tense.

"Something's dripped all over Kevin's gateaux. They're soaked!" Fen cried out.

"They're ruined, aren't they?" Tash whispered.

"It's all my fault. I told you how clumsy I was," said Clarissa, then she sat down in the middle of the floor and burst into tears.

In half a second flat Tash had bobbed down beside her and put her arm round Clarissa's shoulder. "Tell us what happened," she said.

"I was just putting away the French dressing, when Kevin asked me if I'd put the gateau that he'd just finished making into the freezer. There was only one shelf free and that was the top one. I picked up the gateau without bothering to put the French dressing down, but I didn't realize I'd left the top off the dressing and I knocked it against the shelf so it all spilt out."

Fen gasped and Luce started sucking her thumb nail, which she often did when she was watching a film and something awful was about to happen.

"Well, it just poured down through all the shelves, and I've been in torture for the last twenty minutes, wondering how to tell Jan. In the end I chickened out."

Fen and I examined the gateaux in the freezer.

"I'd say the next three down are ruined because they're really soggy," I said, "but the ones underneath may only have the teeniest drop on them so they could possibly be saved."

"You can't really serve a slice of gateau to someone if it smells of vinegar," Luce said. (Luce knows about these things because her mum's a caterer.)

"Right," said Fen, springing into action. "Let's get them out of this freezer and put them in the chest freezer for a few minutes while we thoroughly wipe all these shelves down."

"Come on," Tash said, pulling Clarissa to her feet and thrusting a cloth into her hands. I helped Fen transfer the gateaux while the others pulled out the shelves and wiped them, then we sprayed air freshener in there for good measure.

"Kevin's really nice, isn't he?" Clarissa threw into our industrious silence, which made us all stop and wait to hear what was coming next.

"Yes, he is," we all agreed.

"I mean … couldn't you just explain to Kevin about the gateaux, so Jan need never know?"

Fen frowned and pursed her lips, considering the idea, but her face returned to normal almost immediately. "No chance, Clarissa. Kevin doesn't get here till about eleven o'clock. People often have a slice of cake with their coffee in the morning. Jan'll find out. We can't stop her opening the freezer, can we?"

"These two don't smell too bad," I pointed out. "Let's put them back in the freezer. We'll just have to come clean about the others and explain what happened to Clarissa with the French dressing."

"She'll hate me because I didn't confess at the time," Clarissa said, in a quavering voice.

The rest of us all looked at each other. We

were all thinking the same thing – that Clarissa was trying to get away without confessing at all. Not one of us offered any sympathy, we just put the sparkling clean shelves back into the freezer.

It was then that I remembered there was something I wanted to ask Clarissa. If I didn't ask now, I might never have another opportunity. I didn't really want Fen and Tash listening, but there was no other choice.

"Why does your brother record his phone conversations?" I plunged in, before I lost my nerve.

Chapter 7

Clarissa was taken off her guard. She went red and looked very flustered. Fen looked baffled, which made me realize that Tash hadn't said a word to her best friend about the tape that had dropped out of Peta's dungarees. Good old Tash.

"He ... doesn't..." was Clarissa's lame reply.

"Oh yes he does," Luce objected.

"How do you know?" Clarissa asked.

"Because Tash's little sister brought home the evidence," I informed her.

"So that's where it went," murmured Clarissa.

"So you *did* know," Luce said accusingly.

"He'd kill me if he found out I'd breathed a word about it," Clarissa said with feeling.

"You haven't told us anything we didn't know already," I pointed out. "What we want to know is why he does it?"

"Have you listened to the tape?" Clarissa asked me rather slyly. I nodded. "So you've heard the phone call from Emma Ludgate?" she went on. Again I nodded, though I was well aware of the others all looking at me with great interest. It was at that moment that I pieced together what had been puzzling me.

"I suppose it was you who told Emma Ludgate that I'd be at the drama group, was it?"

"Might have been," Clarissa answered, sticking her chin up stubbornly.

"You still haven't told us why Dom tapes phone conversations," Luce put in impatiently. Clarissa's face took on a very cunning look.

"I'll tell you why on two conditions," she announced, with a sly smile. We waited.

"One – you don't ever let on that it was me

who told you, and two – you don't dob on me to Jan about the vinegar."

I glanced round to see the reactions of the other three. They all nodded. I think they were as curious as I was to find out about Dom and his telephone taping.

"Promise?" Clarissa persisted.

"Promise," we all said in sing-song voices, thinking how babyish this was becoming. Then she explained, and I almost wished I'd never asked.

"Dom and Carl are in a competition. All the boys in their year at Finsbury have got into pairs…" I drew in my breath sharply, while Fen and Tash looked horrified and Luce started frantically chewing on her thumb nail. "…Each pair has put one pound into a central kitty. The winning pair get all the money…"

"But what do they have to do?" Luce squealed.

The redness came rushing back to Clarissa's face.

"Come on, spit it out," Tash said, quite

forcefully for her.

"They have to prove they've been out with more girls than any other pair…"

I felt as though my heart was beating in my throat at that moment, and Luce's features were drenched with sadness.

"…So that nobody can cheat, the boys all made the agreement that they had to provide proof of every single girl they went out with. What they decided on was a tape of a phone conversation between them and the girl, but it didn't count unless the girl had actually phoned *them*. The competition comes to an end today and Dom and Carl were winning, but then they lost their latest tape."

All the time Clarissa was talking, my mind was thinking back over the past few days. So that was why Dom had arranged to be at the café on Monday morning. He must have known from Mum that I would be going round Finsbury Leighton at that time. So he got Carl, his partner in crime, to phone Luce and tell her to make sure I would be there. That way he could guarantee I would phone him back. I played right into his hands. I gave him the phone call he wanted to tape on a silver platter. Oh, why was I so stupid and gullible?

I suddenly remembered I was supposed to be going out with him to the cinema in one hour's time. Huh! He wouldn't be there, of course. He had no need to keep the date, did he? Because, although it was a bit of a setback, losing the tape, he'd managed to get yet another phone call out of me. *"Jaimini, there's someone at the door. Can you phone me back?"* Oh, why was I such a sucker? And then there was that time with Clarissa and Sarah. *"Well, they're friends. We're more partners really."*

It was all falling so horribly into place. Those two boys at the drama class. They were from Finsbury Leighton. I hadn't misheard that sniggery whisper. *"We're only here to beat Dom and Carl."*

I looked at Luce. She had her head in her hands. Nobody felt like talking to Clarissa any more. She seemed like part of the enemy team. But there was one more thing I had to know, however, although I felt so stupid asking.

"I presume there's n-no … rabbit…" I finally stammered, looking at the ground.

"No."

I really hated Clarissa at that moment. I couldn't understand anyone who would cover for their brother when he was being so two-faced.

"Dom makes my life miserable unless I keep his secrets," Clarissa defended herself. "He … pays me … to keep quiet."

"He *pays* you!" Fen screeched. "No wonder you weren't bothered about getting paid for working here," she added, crossly.

"I should have known the moment he came out with that ridiculous name," I said, almost talking to myself.

"He was in the room when you were talking to me about his rabbit that time on the phone," Clarissa explained in a flat voice. "He mouthed 'Beetroot' to me, but I thought he was saying 'Be True'."

So now I knew.

"You promise you won't tell Jan or Dom?"

"Yeah, yeah, yeah," Fen replied in a lazy

voice, as she turned her back on Clarissa. Fen had managed to pick up what was going on and piece it all together. She was obviously really upset on our behalf.

"See you tomorrow, you two," Clarissa said to Luce and me as she was going out of the door.

"You won't see *me*!" Luce called aggressively, just before the door shut and we went to sit in the café.

"So to summarize," I said, cynically. "Dom gets a hilariously entertaining recording of the stupid twit of the year, Jaimini Riva, then he drops me, then when he finds his winning tape is missing, he invites me out again, making sure that I phone him back... *'There's someone at the door. Can you phone me back when you've asked your mum?'* I feel so stupid ... and so angry. How could I have ever even considered going to Finsbury Leighton with or without Dominic Bede? I must have been out of my tiny mind. Andy was right. I must apologize to her the moment I see her."

As I said that, the door between the kitchen

and the café slowly opened, and we all froze.

There stood Andy herself, with Leah. "Sorry," she said, seeing our fright. "We thought we'd come along and see how Clarissa got on."

"But when we saw the time, we thought we'd probably be too late," Leah went on. "Then we heard voices in here and wondered who it could be."

"Look, I'm really sorry I flew at you," I said to Andy.

"That's OK," Andy grinned. "We heard the last part of what you were saying. I gather Dominic Bede is not exactly flavour of the month," she went on.

"And neither is Carl Smythe," Luce added, with feeling. We then proceeded to tell Andy and Leah the whole story, and all about the drama class and everything.

"What was really upsetting us, Jaimes," Andy said at the end, "was that you might have gone off to Finsbury Leighton and left us all behind. I was worried about the Café Club of course, but it wasn't just that … it was *us*… I mean, we're a team, aren't we?" I felt really touched when Andy said that. I smiled and nodded because I didn't trust myself to speak.

"So now we've somehow got to get you both out of doing that exam tomorrow," Fen said.

"It won't be a problem getting me out of it," Luce said. "My parents thought I'd gone stark staring mad when I told them I wanted a shot at it."

"It won't be as easy as that with me," I said sadly. "Mum and Dad are determined that I'm going to Finsbury."

"Couldn't you just skip the entrance exam tomorrow?" Leah suggested.

"Or really boff up the paper?" Tash added.

"It wouldn't do any good. According to Mum I've been offered a place there already, even without doing the test."

"Even with that awful science test you did last Friday?" Luce reminded me with a gleam in her eye.

"I'd forgotten about that," I said rather sheepishly.

"Teachers aren't completely stupid," Andy said. "They'll realize instantly that you were making some kind of statement. You have to be much more subtle than that."

"You mean only boff it up a bit, tomorrow?" Luce asked.

"Yes, nothing too obvious."

"What if I still pass?"

"We'll have to have a serious talk with your parents," Andy said.

"Very serious," Luce agreed whole-heartedly, but nothing anyone said would get rid of my awful fear that I would end up going to Finsbury Leighton, where everyone would snigger and whisper behind their hands about that stupid girl who fell for Dominic Bede's ridiculous excuse about taking his rabbit, Beetroot, to the vet's. It made my face feel red as a beetroot just thinking about it.

"I'd better be going," Tash said.

"Me too," said Fen. "Can you do the lock up, Jaimes?"

"Yeah. Course."

"Everybody think hard tonight," Andy

ordered, "and we'll compare notes tomorrow."

So off went Fen and Tash.

"Can your parents afford the fees at Finsbury?" Andy asked a moment later.

"Not really…" I answered thoughtfully. "In fact, Mum mentioned that she might be going back to nursing. I see why now. It's to help with the fees."

"Right, that's it!" Andy announced excitedly. "All we've got to do is to make sure she can't get a job, then they won't be able to pay for you to go!"

It seemed so obvious, so why was I unconvinced?

"I've got the horrible feeling they may be hoping I'll get a scholarship," I said slowly. "Then they wouldn't have to pay my fees at all. That would explain why Mum was only *thinking* about getting a job. She was waiting to see how well I did in the test."

"Good. That makes it even more important that you don't do anywhere near your best," Andy said.

We all nodded. As we got up to leave things

were looking a little more hopeful. Agreeing to all meet together again the next day after my test, we parted ways.

"Bad luck tomorrow, Jaimes," was Tash's parting shot.

"Oh yes, hope you do really badly," Andy said.

"Yes, fail well," Leah added.

"I can't wait to tell Carl Codface where to get off," was the last thing Luce said to me that day, and I couldn't get those words out of my head all the way home.

Mum was in the kitchen when I went in.

"You're going to be late for the cinema," she said, anxiously.

I'd completely forgotten about my great date with Dom. I was about to say, "I'm not going," when I changed my mind. I *would* go. Of course, I had no intention of keeping the date. I just wanted to see if he was there. I didn't want Mum to think I'd been stood up when I got back though, so this is what I said next.

"I've dumped Dominic Bede."

Mum looked surprised, but just said, "Oh."

Then I made a big thing of fiddling in my pocket. "Oh, no, I've got Luce's earrings in my pocket. I was looking after them for her during drama because they kept catching on her collar. I'll just nip round to her place and give them to her…"

"Yes, all right," Mum said, suspecting nothing at all. So off I went, heart beating, to see whether hateful Dom was keeping our date.

As I approached the cinema I found myself creeping furtively along like a spy. I began to wish I'd asked Andy to do this job, but it was too late by then. I could see the queue from where I was and there was no sign of Dom. He'd probably gone inside. I kicked myself for not thinking this little escapade through first. I couldn't go inside without being seen, but on the other hand I wouldn't know if Dom was there if I didn't.

There was a public phone box about five metres from where I was standing. Reluctantly, I went in and dialled the Bedes'

146

number. Once again Mrs Bede answered.

"Is Dom there, please?" I asked, in a not very good Welsh accent.

"I'm sorry, he's not," Mrs Bede answered. "Who shall I say called him?"

"Gwendolyn," I said, after a quick mental search for a Welsh name.

"All right, I'll tell him you phoned."

"Thank you. Bye bye."

"Bye bye."

I still didn't know if he was at the cinema, but who cared!

Mum was still in the kitchen when I got back.

"Had she missed them?"

"What?"

"The earrings."

"Oh … yes … I mean … no."

I turned to go upstairs but her next words froze me in my tracks.

"You know I mentioned that I might go back to nursing?"

My eyes flew open wide.

"Well, guess what, I've got a job at St

Prestlins! And I'm starting on Monday!"

"Nursing?"

"Yes, isn't it good news? My very first application." She was looking so pleased with herself and all I could do was keep gawping.

"Well, aren't you going to congratulate me?"

"Con…gratu…lations, Mum."

I was completely shell-shocked but managed to mutter something about doing a bit of work upstairs. Then I stumbled out of the kitchen, grabbed the phone from the sitting room, and once in my bedroom dialled Andy's number.

"Allo."

That was Andy's mum, Dominique. She's French and speaks English with a really strong French accent.

"Hello, Dominique, it's Jaimini. Is Andy there, please?"

"I pass you over, Jaimini."

"Hi, Jaimes."

"Hi. Guess what Mum's just announced."

"What?"

"She's got a job at St Prestlins."

"Oh, no! I didn't think she'd get a job

148

organized until she'd heard how you got on in the entrance test."

We both thought about that one for a moment, then I remembered something Luce had said about not boffing up the test too much, not as much as the science test I did last week…

"I bet she's had a bit of feedback from school about my performance on Friday afternoon."

"You're right, that must be it. She's seriously thinking you won't get a scholarship and so she's got the job to pay for the fees."

"Oh Andy, what are we going to do?"

There was a long pause during which I could practically hear Andy's brain cells whirring around.

"I've got it," she finally announced. "I'll phone up St Prestlins, impersonating your mum, and say I can't accept the job after all, then I'll phone your mum, impersonating someone from admin. at St Prestlins and say it's all off."

"What, just like that?"

"Don't worry, I'm not stupid, Jaimini. I can be very convincing when I want to. In fact, better still, I'll get Luce to do it. After all, she's the actress. I'll just write the script."

"We're going to have to move very quickly. Mum's supposed to start work on Monday."

"I'll get on to it tomorrow. Now go and watch tons of television," she finished off jokingly, "and go to bed very late. We want you nice and tired for the exam tomorrow."

I hated going into Finsbury Leighton School for the second time even more than I did the first time. For one thing I kept thinking I might see Dom or Emma. Also I was so determined I wasn't going to go to that school *ever*, it just felt all wrong being on the premises.

There were several of us, all doing the entrance exam in a big hall. I didn't feel nervous at all, just upset that I had to go through with it. I spent the two hours allowed for the paper answering everything rather badly. In between answers I stared into space and thought about Andy's plan to stop Mum going to work, and offered up a few prayers to anyone who might be listening, that we wouldn't be too late.

I was glad when it was all over and I could make my escape. As I was about to go out of the main entrance I saw Carl at the other end of the corridor, walking into one of the classrooms. I waited for a couple of minutes from my safe distance, but there was no sign of Dom anywhere. Part of me was relieved but another part was strangely sad.

Mum was waiting outside to take me home. She was probing hard to find out how easy or difficult I had found the exam. I didn't give much away. The moment we were home I set off for Tash's house where we'd all arranged to meet. I was dying to hear how Andy had got on.

"Hi Jaimes, how did it go?" they all wanted to know the moment I got in through the front door. I sat down and briefly explained that I'd done suitably badly, hadn't seen Dom, but *had* seen Carl in the distance. Luce arranged her features into a look of loathing which was her way of protecting herself from the hurt she felt.

"What about Mum's job, Andy? Did you phone?"

"Not yet, because we thought you might like to hear Luce in action. We've worked out what she's going to say, though, and we've found out from a friend of Tash's mum who your mum would have spoken to at the hospital."

"Oh great, let's get on with it," I giggled. "You *are* sure of what you're going to say, Luce, aren't you? We don't want to blow it, do we?"

"I'm word perfect," Luce said confidently. So Tash went to get the phone and we all sat round while Luce tapped in the hospital number. It was amazing watching her. If it had been me, I would have had to make everyone go out of the room. I would have been as nervous as anything and I would have to have my words in front of me. It would also take me about half an hour to pluck up the courage to make the call.

Luce, on the other hand, was coolly getting

into her role as she tapped in the number. We could actually see her face take on the same expression as Mum's face. It was incredible. Leah did a nervous giggle, but Luce didn't react at all. I don't think she even noticed, she was so deep into what she was about to say.

"Hello. Could I speak to Sonja Davidson?" Pause. "Hello. My name is Brenda Riva. I do apologize for the very short notice, but I'm afraid I'm unable to take up the nursing position I've been offered at St Prestlins because unfortunately my father's just died, and my mother needs a lot of support." (Pause while Luce nodded slowly and gravely two or three times, presumably lapping up the condolences on the other end of the phone.) "I do apologize for any inconvenience I'm causing…" (Pause, presumably while Luce listened to Sonja Davidson protest that of course it was absolutely no inconvenience at all.) "Thank you. That's very kind of you. Yes… Yes, I will… Goodbye."

She put the phone down and we broke into cheers. "That was brilliant, Luce!" and

"Luce, you're a natural!" (My grandad had actually died years before I was born!)

"What did Sonja Davidson say?" I asked.

"She said, 'I'm so sorry to hear your sad news, and of course we quite understand. It's very thoughtful of you to have notified us so quickly. Please don't think for a moment that you've caused any inconvenience. I hope you and your mother get over your sad loss soon.'"

We all clapped and laughed at Luce's brilliant imitation of the woman on the other end of the phone. "Now for the other phone call," Andy said. "This one will be tougher."

But Luce was already dialling my number, so we shut up and waited with bated breath.

After about twenty seconds she replaced the phone. "No reply. I'll try later."

"I guess Mum's gone shopping or something."

I must have been looking really worried because Luce said, "Cheer up Jaimes, you're only a phone call away from sending all thought of going to that hateful school right down the drain!"

"Let's celebrate in the café this afternoon," Tash suggested. "Who's on duty?"

"Me," I said. "And Jan said I could start earlier today."

"Not Andy?"

"Andy's doing tomorrow."

"Lucky you, going early. You'll get more money!" Luce said, wrinkling her nose.

"We'll share the afternoon if you want…"

"No, it's OK. I'm going out to lunch at a posh restaurant with Aunty Edith who is at least ninety-seven in the shade, but never mind, it only happens once every two years!"

"Tash and I are going swimming. Anyone want to join us?" Fen asked.

"I've got to do a load of practising," Leah said, without sounding at all fed up.

"And I've got to look after Sebastien," Andy said, which immediately made me green with envy. Sebastien is so sweet. I'd absolutely love it if I had a little brother like that, or, even better, a little sister like that. Never mind.

"Why don't you come home with me until it's time for you to go to work, Jaimes?" Andy suggested. "You can help me look after Sebastien."

"Oh yes, that would be great," I said, with feeling. I was almost beginning to feel happy – not quite but almost.

Chapter 8

Sebastien greeted us with a loud "PLA!" or at least that's what it sounded like. He stood on his wobbly little legs wearing only a nappy and a T-shirt, and regarded us gravely. Then he yelled out "PLA" again, at the top of his voice. We both giggled, so he repeated it about ten times with a big grin on his face while we giggled even more. Then he walked a few tottery steps, fell back on his padded bottom, got neatly on to all fours, then back up again, wobbled a bit more and fell back on to his bottom for the second time.

At this point he noticed a tiny spot of fluff or something on the floor and completely forgot about us. All his attention went on the fluff. It took him ages to get his finger in exactly the right place to touch it. Concentrating like mad, he finally managed to pick it up and look at it closely. He was just about to put it in his mouth when Andy took it away, which made him scream. She scooped him up and handed him to me. "Look, that's Jaimini." The scream stopped instantly and his eyes went straight to my earrings, which were tiny and sparkly.

For the next ten minutes Sebastien sat happily on my lap examining and fingering first my earrings, then my hair, which he tugged at until I had to unclasp his tiny fingers from it, then my nose, which he pushed and wobbled about while giggling infectiously, then my necklace which he yanked on hard and nearly broke. Finally I put him down and Andy and I surrounded him with toys, thinking, "Right, that'll keep him out of trouble for a while," but all he did was pick them up and throw them wildly around one by one until he was sitting on his own again.

I could have watched him and played with him all day long, but eventually I had to go.

"See you later, Jaimes."

"Yeah. See you."

"Pla!"

I rushed down to the café because I always look forward to working there. I love the bustling atmosphere and it's great to feel like a real part of the adult working world.

So you can imagine my horror when I walked into the kitchen to be met by a stony-faced Jan, who stopped in her tracks when she saw me, and gave me an angry glare.

Of course! The vinegar gateaux! I'd completely forgotten about them. I waited for the onslaught and started to compose some kind of excuse in my head.

"Jaimini, I've got a bone to pick with you," Jan said.

I gulped and was about to launch into a big apology when she completely threw me by saying, "We had a visitor last night..."

"A visitor?"

"A burglar."

"A burglar!"

"Someone walked into this café and stole the contents of the till," she told me.

I clapped my hand to my mouth and felt absolutely sick.

"You may well look ashamed," she said. "I've been on the phone to Fen's mum, and she told me that Fen left you in charge of locking up yesterday evening, and you insisted on transferring the fifty pounds to the safe yourself."

"I'm really sorry, Jan. I don't know how on earth I could have forgotten about it…"

"I know it's not like you. I thought you were the most reliable of the six of you."

"Oh Jan, I'm really sorry. Was it all taken?"

"All fifty pounds, yes."

I thought I was going to faint. I felt so guilty. This was the very worst thing that any of us had ever done since we'd first started working at the café. All sorts of thoughts began spinning round in my head, mainly ideas of how to raise fifty pounds.

"Well, there's nothing more to be done. I've notified the police and they've been to have a look round but nothing else has been taken or touched. They've fingerprinted the till, but unless it's someone with a record who's committed the crime, there's no hope of finding out who it was, or recovering the money."

"I'm really really sorry, Jan," I repeated for the third time. In my mind I started to blame Dom because if I hadn't been so preoccupied with Clarissa's bombshell, I wouldn't have forgotten to transfer the money and lock up.

"Well, I won't say any more about it now, Jaimini. I don't bear grudges, so let's just forget about it."

"OK," I whispered unhappily.

I then set about my work with a vengeance to try and take my mind off the fact that I was responsible for a theft, but no matter how hard I worked I couldn't get that awful news out of my head.

It was about half an hour later when I was clearing one of the tables that I heard a blood-curdling scream from one of the ladies at table eight.

"Aarggh!"

"Whatever's the matter?" Jan asked, whipping over to the table and leaning forward with concern.

"This gateau is contaminated!" the woman declared loudly.

Without further ado, Jan snatched up a clean fork from the next table and tasted a tiny bit of the gateau.

I felt my face getting hot and my knees beginning to shake. Here comes problem number two, I thought. If only I could just blame it on Clarissa, but we'd promised we wouldn't let on that it was her and a promise was a promise. I sighed and waited for the second onslaught.

"Jaimini, could you cut a slice from a different gateau and put this slice in the bin, please? It doesn't taste quite right. I'll have a word with Kevin."

I did as I was told and cut a slice from the other gateau. Surely this one would taste all

right? There may not be any need to say anything at all to Jan. She would mention it to
Kevin. Kevin would be a bit perplexed, but
being a guy of very few words, he'd probably
just shrug his shoulders and say something
like, "Even the best chefs have got to make
the occasional boff!"

I returned with the slice from the other
gateau, smiled sweetly at the displeased
customer, who glared back at me, then went
back to the table I had been clearing. After five
seconds I got the knee trembles again because
she was doing a repeat performance.

"Aarggh! This one is no better. This place
should be shut down – serving gateaux like
these which are unfit for human consumption."

"I'm very sorry, madam," Jan said. "Please
accept something else and another drink for
you and your friend with our compliments."

"I particularly wanted a slice of gateau,"
complained the nauseating lady, loudly.

"I'll find you one, madam. Two seconds."

Uh-oh, I thought. This was curtains. I
followed Jan into the kitchen because there

was no point in putting off the awful confession a moment longer.

"Kevin, what happened to those gateaux you made yesterday? How come most of them are missing and the remaining two are soaked in vinegar?"

"Pass," Kevin answered.

"Well, come and see for yourself," Jan persisted.

Kevin wandered over and looked in the freezer.

"Haven't a clue."

Jan shook her head with bewilderment, then suddenly realized I was standing there. She narrowed her eyes. "I don't suppose you know anything about this, do you, Jaimini?"

"Um…"

"You do, don't you?"

I'd promised Clarissa I wouldn't dob on her, and a promise is a promise. This meant of course, that I had to take the blame myself. I took a deep breath.

"Well, you see, I was just showing Clarissa where the vinegar was kept because she'd forgotten to put it away, you see, when she wanted to show me the gateaux that Kevin had made. She told me that the one on the top was the best, so I stood on tiptoe to see it and put my hands on the shelf, only I forgot I'd still got the vinegar in my hand, and I hadn't realized the top wasn't on … and it tipped over everything."

"So you've known all this time, yet you didn't own up?" Jan asked, as though she couldn't believe what she was hearing.

I nodded miserably and wished I could turn into a fly and fly out of the window into oblivion.

I'll never know what Jan was about to say because the back door opened and in walked Andy, Fen, Leah, Tash and Luce. Jan chose that moment to snap.

"I'm sorry. I've had enough. Off you go, Jaimini. This is just too much for one day. All of you had better go. Go on."

The others looked absolutely gobsmacked. And well they might. They had no idea at all what was going on. All they'd done was walk in through the back door and Jan had totally flipped and sent us all home.

"She'll see the funny side soon," Kevin whispered as I followed the others out. All I could think was, would you laugh if you'd had fifty pounds stolen and you were about to lose at least one good customer? I smiled at him to thank him for being kind, and out we trooped, six silent, humble girls.

"It seems unfair that you should have to take all the blame," Leah commented when I'd finished explaining all that had happened. "I mean, we were all to blame really. It was up to all of us to think about locking up."

"And you shouldn't carry the can for the vinegar mistake, either," Tash went on.

"They're both my fault," I said. "I assured Fen I'd lock up and I assured Jan I'd transfer the money to the safe. As far as the vinegar is concerned, I was the one who wanted to find out about Dom and the taping. There's no reason why anyone else should share the blame."

"No, I think Leah's right," Andy said

staunchly. "I'm going back to tell Jan."

"I shouldn't if I were you," Fen warned her. "I know my aunt almost as well as my mum. She won't want to see any of us till she's calmed down."

"Maybe Kevin will be able to bring her round," Tash said, and we all took meagre grains of comfort from that.

"I'll speak to Mum," Fen said. "I'll try to explain the honest truth to her. After all, we only promised Clarissa we wouldn't tell Jan about the vinegar, we never said anything about not telling *anyone*."

"That's true," said Tash. "Then your mum can explain it all to Jan, and tell her we're all prepared to forfeit our pay until the stolen money is made up."

We all felt slightly cheered up then because Fen's mum and Jan are sisters and they're really close. Also, Fen gets on very well with her mother and her mum is quite understanding, as mothers go.

"If we'd never met Dodo and Codface, none of this would have happened," Luce commented, angrily. Normally a remark like this would have made us at least giggle, but on this occasion nobody reacted at all.

At home, I sat and watched television while waiting for Fen's phone call to tell me how she'd got on with telling her mum everything. I grabbed the phone when it rang and belted up to my room with it when I heard that it was Fen. She was speaking very softly as though afraid that her mum might hear her.

"It's not very good news, I'm afraid," she began. "Apparently Jan's absolutely furious, and Mum is completely siding with her and refusing to even put our side of the argument to her. She says she agrees with Jan that it was the height of irresponsibility to leave the café without locking up. When I tried to defend us by going on about Dom and the taping, she said that Jan wouldn't have forgotten to transfer money to the safe and lock up even if she'd just had to tackle a grizzly bear single-handed, and was still trembling from the experience…"

My spirits were almost at rock bottom. I knew Fen was leaving something out. I could just tell.

"What else did she say, Fen?"

"She said … she said that Jan was thinking of sacking the lot of us, or … or she may just sack you."

The tears stung my eyes and my throat began to hurt as I finally did hit rock bottom.

"Don't worry, though, Jaimes, because if she sacks you, we'll all come out in sympathy and refuse to work unless you're reinstated."

"Then she'd get mad and sack you all anyway," I pointed out. "Oh, Fen, it's all my fault. I just don't know what to do."

"Don't do anything," Fen said. "I know Mum. She's all upset on Jan's behalf. It's because they're so close. I'll give her twenty-four hours to calm down, then I'll have another go at her."

"Thanks, Fen. You're a real friend."

"Try not to worry, Jaimes. See you tomorrow. OK?"

"Yeah, see you."

When I'd put the phone down I had a long think. There was one very obvious thing I could do to make everything better. I'd write to Jan, handing in my resignation. That way Jan wouldn't have any choice to make. The others could keep their jobs, and I wouldn't feel guilty any more. After all, both Clarissa and the robbery were *my* responsibility and mine alone.

I sat down at my desk and composed a letter. After several efforts which I screwed up and chucked in the bin, this is what I eventually came up with.

Dear Jan,

I can never apologize enough for being the cause of last night's robbery and your loss of fifty pounds. I'm also really sorry about the gateaux. Both these matters have got nothing at all to do with any of the others. I'm going to Finsbury Leighton School next term so I won't be able to continue working at the café. I know the others are keen to continue, though, and they have a replacement in mind for me, who is a very reliable girl. Thank you for all your past kindness to me.

With best wishes,

Jaimini

I had made up the bit about Finsbury, although, as it happened, perhaps it would be better all round if I *did* go there. I was actually past caring *where* I went by then.

I'd also made up the bit about the replacement for me, but I wanted to write something that would encourage Jan to keep everything going with the rest of the girls so they wouldn't suffer because of my stupidity.

I stamped and addressed the envelope and went down to Mum. "I'm just going to post this letter, Mum."

"Oh, all right. Could you post this one for me too, please?" I took it from her and walked down to the post box which was only a few minutes away.

My hand, holding the two letters, hovered over the opening in the post box, then I quickly dropped them in. If only I'd looked at the address on the one from Mum. But I hadn't and it was too late.

Mum was somehow very edgy when I got back and installed myself in front of the television. She seemed to want to talk. Personally, I just wanted to lose myself in a good film or something and try to forget the awful position I was in.

"I met Jean Wood today in town," said Mum.

"Mm." I didn't think anything about Jean Wood warranted more than a token grunt from me, because I hardly knew her at all, and Mum didn't really know her much better. She worked part time in the library and had grown-up children, that's all I knew.

"She was telling me about Dominic."

This time I paid more attention, but tried to keep my voice suitably lazy. "What about him?"

"Did you know he's in hospital?"

"In hospital?" There was no denying she had my full attention now.

"Apparently he was hit by a car early

yesterday evening."

My mind was doing somersaults. Was it on his way to meet me? I started to feel anxious. "Is … is he OK?"

"He's still unconscious. At least he was this morning when I spoke to Jean."

My mouth felt dry. I didn't really know what to say, because I didn't really know how I felt. Mum must have sensed my anxiety and confusion. "He's going to be all right, love. It's just a question of waiting for him to come round."

"But what happened?"

"I don't know exactly … Jean wasn't too sure … but…"

"But what?"

"Well … he was knocked down near the café… And apparently a boy answering Dom's description was seen leaving the café round about that time… Unfortunately, people are now starting to link Dom with the theft that happened at the café that evening…"

"Dom? A thief!"

Mum paused and her eyes did this darting

about thing that they do when she's nervous. I realized why with her next words.

"You didn't mention that the café had been burgled, Jaimini? Why not?" she asked gently, but with a hint of what I suppose was disappointment in me.

I sighed and closed my eyes while I asked myself, "Should I tell her?" Then before I knew it I was pouring it all out to her. Well, not quite everything. I didn't tell her about Dom and Carl's stupid competition or anything – just that I had dumped Dom and was so wrapped up with wondering whether or not I'd done the right thing, that I completely forgot to transfer the money and to lock up.

Mum's eyes opened wider and wider as I told her all this, and when I'd finished I could tell she was stuck for words. She thought she ought to be telling me off, but then there was no point because I'd apologized and I'd handed in my resignation.

"Oh … love," she said eventually, as she put a comforting arm round my shoulder. She didn't even add, "Perhaps Jan'll let you off the hook," or anything like that, which showed how seriously she viewed the whole thing.

"Which hospital is he at?"

"The Cableden Central."

"I think I'll bike over there."

"What, now?"

"Yes."

"But…"

I was out of the room. I grabbed my coat and helmet and made for the front door.

"I was going to talk to you about Finsbury…"

"What?" I shouted, because by then I was outside our front gate.

"I've returned the form…"

I didn't hear the rest of the sentence because a big lorry chose that moment to go by. It didn't make any difference, anyway. Finsbury Leighton was the last thing on my mind.

"Please let him have come round. Please let him have come round," I said over and over again as I pedalled fast towards the hospital.

I realized when I got there that I had no idea

at all where to find Dom, or even if I would be allowed in to see him. I headed towards reception but before I got there someone called out to me.

"Hi, Jaimini." I turned to see Carl, looking pale under his freckles. "Come to see Dom?"

"Yes. Has he regained consciousness?"

"No, but he's out of intensive care, I'm just going up there."

We went up the three flights of stairs without saying a word. I was frantically trying to think of some good conversation opener, but whichever words formed in my brain, I couldn't voice them because the whole situation was so embarrassing. Anyway, I had to keep reminding myself that I hated Dom's guts, but it's difficult to hate someone's guts when they're lying unconscious in a hospital bed.

We walked into the little side ward together. There were curtains all round Dom's bed. The sister obviously knew Carl because she smiled and said, "Hello," then walked off. I followed Carl through the opening in the curtains, and saw Dom. He was still un-conscious. That made it even more difficult to strike up a conversation with Carl. There was simply nothing to say. We looked at each other.

"I usually just sit here and say a few things, you know," he said, shuffling his feet and looking down. At that moment in time, I liked Carl more than ever before or since.

"I'll leave you to it, then," I said, with a flicker of a smile. "Oh … and if he does wake up, could you mention that I was here?"

"Yes. Course."

I rang Luce from the public phone box in the hospital because I suddenly felt the need to talk to someone close to me. She was as shocked as I had been. I told her what Carl had said, and she went quiet. Like me she was probably trying to fit the image of the hateful "girl collector" to the boy who was trying to talk his friend back to the land of the living.

I went on to tell Luce in a flat voice that mum had sent the form to Finsbury.

"She *what*!"

"Sent the form to Finsbury."

"Jaimes, how can you tell me so calmly? If that form gets into the hands of the registrar, there'll be no turning back!"

"It's probably the best place for me to be, Luce. Then I can't make any more cock-ups at the café."

"Oh, Jaimini, have you gone totally bonkers or something? You are *not* going to that school and that is *that*. Right. Action! When did your mum send the letter?"

"It must have been this afternoon. I posted it, but I didn't bother to look at the address. She told me just before I came here to the hospital."

"First thing in the morning, I'm going to Finsbury Smelly Leighton to waylay the postman. I'll do a hold-up on the post van if necessary. Oh, Jaimes, you don't half make it hard work, being your best friend. I've got to go now. I need to get my beauty sleep if I'm to be up with the lark."

With that she rang off and I pedalled back

home, my mind spinning with phrases I'd heard during the day…

Apparently he was hit by a car early yesterday evening… People are starting to link him with the theft that happened at the café… I was going to talk to you about Finsbury… I've returned the form… I usually sit here and say a few things… You don't half make it hard work, being your best friend.

Dad was home by the time I got back from the hospital. Like Mum, he seemed in the mood for talking, but I didn't feel like saying more than a few words about how I'd seen Dom and he hadn't regained consciousness. Neither Mum nor Dad seemed surprised when I said I was going to bed early. The truth was I just wanted to get rid of that horrible day and start another one. After all, it couldn't be worse than the one I'd just been through.

Chapter 9

I spent a restless night, and when I did manage to sleep I had weird dreams about giants with stockings pulled over their faces, firing guns in a hospital operating theatre and calling out in threatening voices, "Your money or your life!" In the worst dream of all, the person on the operating table suddenly sat up and I saw that they had no head, and yet a voice which sounded like Dom's was calling out, "I'll take the money."

I woke up with a jolt and sat bolt upright, shaking in terror. I felt wide awake, and anyway there was no way I was going back to sleep in case I had a repeat nightmare. I looked at my alarm clock. It said six-thirty-five, so I got up, washed and dressed and went downstairs.

"This is a rare treat," smiled Dad as I went into the kitchen.

He and Mum were drinking coffee and eating toast. The radio was on and it was a lovely cosy atmosphere. I sat down and joined them, yawning a bit.

"I've had bad dreams all night long," I told them.

"Well, let's hope they're well and truly out of your system now," Mum said. "Want a cup of tea?"

I nodded and yawned again.

"So what do you think of our decision, then?" Dad asked me, leaning forwards and smiling.

"What decision?"

"About Finsbury. Mum told you yesterday evening, I gather."

"I wasn't surprised… I knew how much you wanted me to go there."

Mum and Dad were looking at each other in a very puzzled way.

"So, why weren't you surprised that we changed our minds?"

"You what?!"

"You *did* tell her, Brenda?"

Mum nodded, a slow puzzled nod, and into my head came a picture of me on my bike just outside our gate, and a big lorry going past.

"I didn't hear what you said. There was this lorry going by and…"

"Well, we knew you were dead against the idea, and then your head teacher phoned up and told us what a deliberate mess you'd made of the science test, and advised us not to be too hasty. She said that for a bright, well-adjusted girl like you to make such a very strong statement as you did in that test, you must be desperate not to be uprooted…"

"Are you saying I don't have to go there?" I asked, jumping up.

"Exactly," Mum answered, looking delighted that I was so ecstatic. "I posted the form yesterday to say that we're not accepting the place. They should get it this morning." She beamed broadly.

"Omigod!"

"Whatever's the matter now?"

"I'll explain later," I called out, because by then I was out of the house and on my bike.

"Please be too late, Luce," I said over and over again as I pedalled along. It occurred to me that if anyone had been watching me last night and this morning, they'd think I'd gone out of my tiny mind, talking to myself while zooming along at top speed on a rather cranky bike.

When I arrived at Finsbury it was seven-forty-five. There wasn't much sign of life, except for two cars parked immediately outside the main entrance. The window of the school office looked out on to the drive so I veered off to the left and hid my bike behind a hedge, then sneaked cautiously back into the drive keeping as close into the hedge as I could.

I wondered where Luce could be. That was the problem – the fact that I didn't know where she was. If she'd already gone in, I had to follow her. On the other hand she might have overslept, in which case I didn't want to go to all the trouble of making up a suitably convincing story for the registrar. I decided there was nothing for it, I'd just have to go in.

With every step I took on the polished wooden floor, my trainers squeaked, and I was surprised I made it as far as the school office without anyone stopping me on the grounds of noise pollution. I knocked on the door and went in when no one answered.

A lady who was presumably the school secretary was typing away with what looked like a Walkman on. It must have been one of those dictaphones which would explain why she hadn't heard me knock. I walked up to her desk which made her jump.

"Oh, I didn't hear anyone come in," she said, removing the earphones and looking surprised.

"I'm sorry to disturb you," I began, "but I was here yesterday, doing an exam, and I think I must have left my pencil case behind. It's got some money in it, so as soon as I noticed it was missing, I thought I'd better come straight away and retrieve it."

She was looking full of concern. "Oh, dear... I don't think a pencil case has been handed in at all. Would you just wait here a moment while I go and make enquiries, please?"

"Yes, of course."

Perfect! She had said and done precisely what I'd hoped she would. The moment she'd gone out I set to work. There were unopened and opened letters on her desk, and more in a shallow basket on another desk, and yet more on a third desk which said REGISTRAR on it. Aha! I rummaged through all those letters first and there was no sign of Mum's letter, so I began on the letters in the little basket, but then I heard footsteps coming back, so I sat down again and composed my features.

"No luck, I'm afraid," the lady said, still full of concern. I wished I could tell her not to worry, because it was all made up, she looked so sorry for me, but I just smiled and said, "I expect I must have dropped it somewhere else, then. Thanks for your help, anyway."

I turned towards the door, but stopped and turned back when she said, "It's quite a day for early morning visitors."

"Oh … am I not the first?" I asked, trying not to sound too curious.

"No, there was a *very* strange girl here a few minutes ago."

Oh, dear. What excuse had Luce dreamt up for gaining entry?

"She started spouting all this stuff from the Bible – most peculiar. I had to get help to make her leave the premises…"

As she had been talking I'd had a job not laughing at the picture that was forming in my mind of Luce filled with religious fervour and trying to convert the school secretary, who looked a very ordinary and unpassionate sort of person.

"I'd better be going," I said. "I hope you don't get any more disturbances."

"Never mind, it all serves to make my day more interesting," she smiled, before popping the dictaphone back on and resuming her typing.

I rushed off to Luce's house next and I must have gone amazingly quickly, or otherwise she'd gone very slowly, because she was only just getting off her bike as I rode up.

"Jaimini, what are you doing here?"

"Come to join your Bible class," I joked.

"How did you know about that?" she grinned, but looked suitably impressed.

I told her all that happened to me since waking up, and watched her expression go from ecstatic to worried to neutral as she reached into her inside jacket pocket.

"Da-da!" she said, like a magician producing a rabbit from a hat. And then her face dropped a mile because there was nothing in her hand. She began a deranged sort of search of all her pockets, her eyes growing more and more panicky. I waited with bated breath, willing Mum's letter to suddenly appear. In the end, Luce took off her jacket and shook it out, then turned her jeans pockets inside out. Nothing.

"But I had it, I definitely had it," she cried, still ramming her hands into all her pockets frantically. "I recognized your mum's handwriting instantly. At some point I transferred it from my pocket to the inside of my jacket so it wouldn't get crumpled…"

"I'll just have to explain it all to Mum and get her to write another one," I said, thoughtfully.

"What if it's too late by the time they get her next letter?" Luce said, with rising panic.

"We'd better retrace your footsteps all the way back to Finsbury," I said.

"You mean, my pedals."

So off we set. It was a slow journey because we had to keep an eye on the other side of the road, where Luce would have cycled on her way back home. It wasn't easy to do this without wobbling and almost hitting the kerb every five seconds.

"It's no good," Luce sighed when we were nearly there.

"Are you certain you had it when you left the main gate?" I pressed her.

"I'm certain I had it when I came out of the building," she said hesitantly, "but I suppose

I'm not all that certain where I was exactly when I transferred it to my jacket."

"We'll have to go in."

"We can't. Look."

I looked, and saw immediately what Luce's concern was. All around there were Finsbury girls and boys arriving for school.

"Let's wait a few minutes till there aren't so many, then go in."

"Someone's sure to have picked it up and taken it in, aren't they?"

"I suppose so. But what if they haven't? I mean, we can't rely on it, can we?"

So we hung about patiently for roughly five minutes, then when there were only very few pupils about, in we went, walking our bikes slowly and scanning the ground all around intently. It came as quite a shock when my eyes alighted on some eighteen-hole DM boots, right in front of my front tyre. I followed the boots and the legs up, and came face to face with Emma Ludgate. In her hand she held Mum's letter. Her hate-filled eyes appraised me coolly.

"Just look what one of my friends happened to come across in the school drive this morning," she said, wafting Mum's letter backwards and forwards.

"I'll have that, thank you," I said to her, going for my most authoritative voice, but shaking underneath.

"Uh-uh, not so fast," she said, smiling with great enjoyment at my obvious discomfort.

"Hand it over, Emma," Luce said, "and do try to stop being so catty at least for one minute." Emma's eyes glinted dangerously.

"I see you're not coming to Finsbury," she said, pulling Mum's already opened letter out of the envelope. The indignation I felt that she'd had the cheek to open Mum's letter must have shown in my eyes. She smiled again, no doubt feeling back in control once more. "It doesn't surprise me one little bit, Jaimini, because it would be so embarrassing for you, wouldn't it, now that Dom's back with me again?"

"What do you mean?"

She suddenly looked really smug. "Oh, you

don't know of course, do you? He asked me ... well, begged me actually ... to go back out with him on Wednesday, just before his accident."

"Don't listen to her," Luce interrupted. "Anyway, you're not interested in Dominic Bede, are you Jaimes?"

"N–no, I'm not," I said, with as much conviction as I could muster.

"Hey! Get off!" Emma yelled suddenly, because Luce, quick as a flash, had grabbed the letter from her.

"Impressive!" I congratulated Luce, as we got on our bikes and turned to go. Emma's face looked like thunder.

"I'll get you back, Jaimini Riva!" she called out after us. "You'll regret you ever set eyes on Dominic Bede."

I saw Luce's hackles rise. She was about to retaliate.

"Leave it, Luce. She's still jealous about Dominic swapping her for me. She'll get over it."

So we left the premises and waited for two

or three minutes after the bell, then I took my courage in both hands and entered the awful school for the third time that day. Once inside the building I quickly made my way to the school office. There was not a soul about, not even in the office at that moment, so I placed the letter right in the middle of the registrar's desk, and crept out as fast as I could.

"Done it?" Luce asked me a minute later. I nodded and we set off home, pedalling maniacally as though a pack of wolves was after us.

Neither Mum nor Dad were at home when we got back, which was a relief because it meant that I didn't have to bother with any explanations.

"I wonder if Dom's regained consciousness," I said as I made hot chocolate for Luce and me. Then the phone rang, so Luce took over the hot chocolate making.

"Hello."

"Hi, Jaimini."

"Hi, Fen."

"Guess what?"

"What?"

"Sally Ahlers phoned and I've got the part of Riz!"

"That's great, Fen. Well done!"

"Mum's refusing to talk about the café, I'm afraid, but I reckon she needs a bit more time. Andy is just going to turn up this afternoon as though nothing has happened, and get on with her work."

"She's brave."

"There's nothing else she can do, really."

"I've got one bit of good news... I'm not going to Finsbury, after all."

"Mega! How did that happen?"

"Mum and Dad just realized how dead against the idea I was, so they changed their minds."

"Oh, that's absolutely brilliant, Jaimes! There's hope for grown-ups yet!"

We agreed that Fen would phone me if there were any developments on the café front and meanwhile we'd both cross every finger and every toe. I didn't tell her about the letter I'd written to Jan, because I hadn't even told Luce about that.

Once Luce and I were nicely installed in front of the television with our hot chocolate, I thought it was time I told her about my letter. I was on the point of opening my mouth when I remembered how she'd reacted to the news that I would be going to Finsbury. If I told her about my resignation, who knew what she'd do? All I knew was that it would be something impulsive, and something that may make matters even worse.

No, I'd keep the fact that I'd written to Jan to myself for the time being. After all, it wouldn't be long before Luce and all the others would know, because Jan would get her letter today, and she'd want to be introduced to the new Café Club member – my replacement. I swallowed hard.

Mum came in a few minutes later and she'd hardly walked through the door when the bell rang. I jumped up to answer it. Imagine my horror when I saw a policeman and a policewoman standing there.

"Miss Jaimini Riva?" asked the policeman, without smiling at all.

"Y-yes."

"Is your mother here at the moment?"

"Y-yes."

Mum appeared behind me. "Oh!" was all she said, in a squeaky voice.

"We're sorry to disturb you, Mrs Riva, but we'd like to talk to your daughter, and we'd appreciate your presence during the interview."

"C-come in." Mum turned her worried eyes to me. "Do you know what this is about, Jaimini?"

"Maybe it's about Dom," I whispered.

Luce looked absolutely gobsmacked when I came back into the room with Mum and two police officers.

"This is Lucy Edmunson, Jaimini's friend," Mum explained.

The officers nodded at her and Mum gestured to them to sit down. I sat down too before I collapsed, my legs were shaking so much. The woman police officer took out a note pad and pen as the man began to question me.

"You are aware that the café where you work was burgled on Wednesday evening?"

"Y-yes."

"The manageress, Mrs Geeson, tells us that you were responsible for the lock up that day, but that for some reason you failed to do it."

"It's because I'd just heard some news that had given me a shock, and that put the lock up right out of my mind... I've already explained that to Jan..."

"You may not be aware of it, but the jeweller's next door to the café was also robbed on Wednesday evening..."

"No, I didn't know that. Did you, Mum?"

"Well, Jean Wood mentioned it, but I'm afraid I didn't take much notice because I was so shocked about the café."

"Until now we have been following a certain line of inquiry in connection with both burglaries, that of the getaway vehicle. But today another witness has come forward. This person spotted someone she knew called

Dominic Bede, entering the café on Wednesday at about six-thirty."

I nodded and tried to swallow but couldn't because my mouth was too dry. Luce was sitting so still, you could have mistaken her for a waxwork. I dreaded hearing another word of this awful account of Wednesday evening.

"We are told by this witness that you are Dominic Bede's girlfriend. Is this correct?"

"I – we – not any more…"

"Since when?"

"We-Wednesday evening."

"Hm. I see."

Mum was wringing her hands and looking deathly pale. I guessed I must have looked the same. I felt sick. How could I explain to these police officers that I really *had* decided to dump Dom at six o'clock, precisely half an hour before he was seen entering the café? It all sounded far too much of a coincidence.

"Now, it occurs to us, Miss Riva, that you and your boyfriend may have worked out this clever little plan together. *You* leave the café unlocked, *he* breezes in and takes the contents of the till."

"No! I don't know anything about it. I promise. I'd never do anything like that. Ask Jan…"

"We've spoken to Mrs Geeson, as I say."

I could have cried at that point. Every single thing was against me. It was no wonder I was a suspect.

Luce suddenly came to life. "You've got it all wrong," she cried, leaping to her feet and looking as though she was about to attack the officers. "Dominic Bede was playing a nasty mean trick on Jaimini. She only found out about it at six o'clock on Wednesday. I know, I was there too. She was shocked. We all were. It's no wonder she forgot about locking up. We all did. It was going to be one of the others locking up, but at the last minute she asked Jaimini to do it. Are you saying we're all in it? All six of us? Hmm?"

I could have hugged Luce. She was saying all the right things, even if she was sounding rather rude about it.

"We're just making inquiries, miss. We appreciate that you want to help your friend…"

"I wonder if Dom's regained consciousness yet," Mum murmured.

"We contacted the hospital immediately before coming here, Mrs Riva. That's our next port of call. The boy regained consciousness about half an hour ago. We have permission from the doctor to interview him. We're particularly interested to find out how he came to have the contents of the café's till in his possession."

I gulped. Luce's mouth fell open. Mum's eyes widened. The officer raised his eyebrows and the policewoman snapped shut her notebook. The next few seconds seem to take place in slow motion.

"We'll see ourselves out, Mrs Riva."

"That's all right." Mum got up a bit shakily and opened the front door for them, then she returned to the sitting room and the three of us sat in exhausted silence for about twenty seconds before Luce suddenly shot up and ran out of the front door. She left the door open and we could hear her yelling. "What was her name? What was her name?"

"Whatever is Luce talking about now?" Mum asked, in a tired voice.

She wasn't really expecting an answer. We lapsed back into our weary silence until Luce burst in again and said, "I knew it! I absolutely knew it!"

"Knew what?"

"Guess who this key witness that's come forward is?" she asked, in a voice filled with contempt.

"Tell me."

"Emma Ludgate."

"Emma Ludgate ... of course!" I thought back to her parting shout.

"You'll regret you ever set eyes on Dominic Bede."

"I never thought she'd go to these lengths," I whispered in horror.

"Who's Emma Ludgate?" Mum asked me fearfully.

"A stupid, jealous girl from Finsbury Leighton," Luce explained, rather vehemently.

I felt more perplexed and worried than ever. "But it still doesn't explain how Dom came to have the money on him. And what about the van that knocked him down? Isn't anybody doing anything about that?"

"The police did say they were pursuing that line of inquiry," Mum reminded me.

"Did Jean Wood say anything else about the robbery at the jeweller's?" I asked Mum, in a desperate attempt to piece together some facts.

"Only that it was a very professional job but not much was taken. Just as though the robbers had been interrupted or something."

After another few minutes of morbid contemplation of my fate, Luce jumped up again and dragged me off to my room saying she wanted to listen to the recording of Emma's voice.

As soon as we'd heard Emma's last words, Luce said, "Well, if that's a proper witness, I must be Princess Di. Come on Jaimes, we're going to catch up with those two charming officers and play them this tape. That'll give that policewoman something worthwhile to write in her notebook. It's perfectly obvious to anyone that Emma is out to get you."

I allowed myself to be dragged out of the house by Luce, because I didn't have the energy to protest, and Mum didn't have the energy to stop us going.

I had a job keeping up. Luce kept on calling out to me over her shoulder to hurry up because "we don't want to miss them, do we?"

Once at the hospital we parked our bikes and ran up to the side ward where Dom had been, but the bed was empty and the ward very obviously no longer occupied.

"Can I help you?" asked the same sister who had said hello to Carl the previous day.

"We were looking for Dominic Bede."

"Oh, he's gone home ... good as new!" she added, with a big smile.

"Did some police officers come here?" Luce asked.

"I believe they're meeting Dominic at his home."

Luce seemed deflated to hear this news. As

for me, I was tired out. "I can't be bothered to go to the Bedes' house, Luce. Let's just go home."

So we did, and much more slowly than we'd cycled to the hospital.

Chapter 10

"Jan phoned," Mum said the moment we got in. "She seemed very anxious to talk to you."

I bet she did, I thought wearily. And that's when I decided to tell Luce about the letter I'd written.

"Oh, Jaimes, you nutter," was Luce's response. "I'll stick up for you through thick and thin, and I know the others will too. Either we have a Café Club with all of us, or we don't have one at all. It's as simple as that. Come on, you'd better face the music."

So off we went. Luce practically had to drag me along, because I was so nervous about facing Jan. "Maybe I ought to stay at home in case the police want to get in touch with me," I said.

"Stop making excuses," Luce replied.

We were surprised to see the CLOSED sign on the door of the café. My nervousness doubled then, because I felt responsible for all these dramatic goings on. Luce pushed me in through the back door, but Jan wasn't in the kitchen. In fact the kitchen was completely empty. We leaned cautiously against the swing door and went through to the café. Jan was sitting at one of the tables wiping menus.

I didn't know what to say, and neither did she appear to, but Luce certainly did.

"That letter that Jaimini sent you, have you read it yet?"

"Only just. I forgot about it until now with everything else that's been going on."

"Well, she shouldn't have written it. What have you done with it?" Luce was sounding very no-nonsense and almost aggressive.

"I haven't done anything with it. It's here." And Jan held it up as if to prove her point.

"Well, what *are* you going to do about it?" Luce demanded, while I waited like a little girl who was about to hear what her punishment was to be.

"I'm going to do *this* with it." And Jan slowly ripped the letter in half, then in quarters, then scrumpled it up and put it in the bin.

Luce and I couldn't conceal our surprise. Neither of us was expecting this reaction from Jan.

"You're surely not going to Finsbury Leighton, are you Jaimini?" she asked quietly, looking at me properly for the first time since we'd turned up.

I shook my head and her whole face broke into a big smile of relief.

"Thank goodness for that, because there's no way anyone else is going to take your place. Either I have my same six girls or I don't have anyone."

"That's exactly what I said," Luce said, but it came out sounding really funny because she was expecting a big argument with Jan, and here was Jan totally agreeing with her and repeating the very words she had spoken earlier. It was all very confusing. I managed at last to utter one word.

"Why?"

"Come and sit down, and I'll tell you," Jan said.

So we sat down and listened in amazement as she unfolded this incredible tale.

"I've just got back from Dominic Bede's house," Jan began. "His mother phoned me to tell me that the police were at the house and wanted to see me. Dominic seems to have made a complete recovery, by the way…" She paused and gave me a smile. I made a non-committal noise, because though I was glad he'd recovered, I couldn't feel any sympathy for him.

"Dom was very anxious to talk to me," Jan went on, "but the first thing he did was hand over the fifty pounds from the till. I didn't say a single word to him. In fact I was wondering how he had the audacity to calmly return the money that he'd stolen from me. The policewoman saw the look on my face and said, 'Hear him out, Mrs Geeson.' So I did and this is what he told me:

"He said that on Wednesday his sister, Clarissa, came home from the café and accidentally spilt his Tippex refill tube all over his desk and school books. Dom got mad at her and a big argument broke out between the two of them. Clarissa's last words before she stomped off were, 'Anyway, I've told Jaimini about your stupid competition with the rest of the boys in your class, and she thinks you're pathetic!' Apparently Dom went mad when she said that and demanded to know why on earth she'd broken her promise to him."

At this point Luce and I gave each other knowing looks, then turned back to Jan who carried on, "So that's when Clarissa told Dom how she'd inadvertently tipped a bottle of wine vinegar over Kevin's gateaux, and that Jaimini and the other girls had said they wouldn't tell Jan who had done it as long as Clarissa spilled the beans about why Dom recorded his phone conversations.

"Dom said he felt really guilty because one of you six was inevitably going to get the blame for the vinegar spillage. He guessed it would be you, Jaimini, so he decided to come down to the café to try and find you and patch things up, because he said he'd already abandoned the idea of the competition anyway…"

"Why?" interrupted Luce.

"That I don't know," Jan replied. "Anyway, as he approached the café he thought he saw a man in the jeweller's. He only caught a glimpse of the person, but had a hunch that he was up to no good. So he quickly nipped round to the back of the café to warn you. Of course, when he went into the café through the back door, which wasn't locked, he saw immediately that no one was there, but he couldn't lock the door because you'd taken the key with you.

"With great presence of mind, he decided to take the contents of the till with him, so that no one could steal it, then he went back out and headed to your house to tell you the place wasn't locked up. He didn't know where I lived, or he would have come directly to me, he said.

"When he got outside the first thing he saw was a girl who is always pestering him, called Emma Ludgate. He guessed she was spying on him because she tried to hide in a shop doorway when he looked over in her direction. Anyway, he then forgot all about Emma because the man he had seen came rushing out of the jeweller's and jumped into a white van where the driver was waiting to make a rapid getaway. Dom got a good look at the first man, and also memorized the registration plate as the van accelerated down the High Street, in the opposite direction.

"Wasting no time at all, he then started running towards your house, Jaimini, but he'd gone hardly any distance at all, and was crossing the road, when something roared up to him and knocked him down. He just caught a glimpse of the white van before he blacked out completely, and the next thing he knew, he was waking up two days later in a hospital bed."

"The white van came back deliberately to knock him down?" breathed Luce.

"The police say it looks that way, probably because they knew Dom had seen them and would be a witness to the crime…"

"What about Emma Ludgate, the other witness?" I asked.

"Huh! She was just a troublemaker. Luckily Dom was able to explain to the police what a manipulative piece of work that girl is, and Emma is now in a lot of trouble for wasting police time," Jan told us, and I can't say I felt a shred of sympathy for Emma, and neither, judging from the expression of satisfaction on her face, did Luce.

Jan sat back in her chair and looked at us. I was speechless, and so, for once, was Luce. The phone rang, cutting harshly into our silence.

"Hello," said Jan into the mouthpiece.

There was a pause, and then she handed the phone to me. "It's your mum."

"Hi, Mum."

"The police are here, Jaimini, and it's all right because…"

"Yes, I know, Mum. Jan's just told me the whole story."

"Has she told you that they've caught the robbers?"

"No!"

"Just a few minutes ago – and all because of Dom remembering the registration plate, and what the robber looked like."

"Thank goodness for that!"

"Are you coming home now, Jaimini?"

"Yes, in a few minutes." Something in Mum's voice made me ask her if she was all right.

"Yes, I'm fine," she answered. "I'm just rather tired and ought to go to bed really, but I wanted to talk to you first, now all these dramatic goings on have been sorted out."

There was something about what she had just said which didn't sound quite right, but I couldn't quite put my finger on what it was. I was just about to ring off when a dreadful thought came hurtling into my mind.

"What do you mean, you 'ought' to go to bed, Mum?"

"Well, I'm starting work on Monday, remember…"

"On … Mon…! I'll be home in no time at all," I gasped, before putting the phone down and turning anguished eyes on Luce.

"You know what we've forgotten to do, don't you, Luce?"

She knitted her eyebrows together and looked very puzzled.

"We've forgotten to make the phone call from St Prestlins to Mum, telling her the job is off!"

"Omigod!" Luce leapt up so fast her chair fell over. "I'll phone her now … from here…"

"It's too late now, Luce," I said despairingly.

Jan had been eyeing us curiously for the last couple of minutes. "Well, I don't know what this latest scrape is that you've got yourselves into," she said, "but I suggest you get home and try to sort it out. Come on, I'll give you a lift... And Jaimini, if there's anything I can do to help you out, just give me a shout."

I smiled at her and she put her arm round my shoulders. "I don't know, you girls don't half land yourselves in some ridiculous situations."

She was right. And this time we were well and truly landed.

Jan dropped Luce off first and then me. I thanked her for the lift and stood by our gate waving her off because I was putting off the awful moment when I had to tell Mum what we'd done.

When Jan's little Renault had disappeared round the corner, I finally turned towards the house, but turned round immediately at the sound of my name.

"Jaimini."

It was Emma Ludgate wearing her usual hateful expression.

"I hear you're in a bit of trouble for telling lies, Emma," I said smoothly.

"And I hear Dom made a complete fool out

214

of you," she retorted with a sneer. "I know all about the taping, you see, Jaimini. Another Finsbury boy told me." She started to snigger. "Fancy thinking that anyone has got a rabbit called Beetroot. It's the funniest thing I've ever heard – and all my friends agree. I'm not surprised you're not coming to Finsbury. You'd never be able to hold your head up now everybody knows how gullible you are. Anyway, I just popped round to tell you that Dom won't take long to come back to me. He's done this before you know, but in the end he always comes back to me because I'm so much more mature than girls like you…"

She broke off abruptly and seemed to be struck dumb by something behind me. I turned and there, coming out of my front door, was Dom. Loads of questions formed on my lips, but none of them was voiced because Dom spoke first.

"You never stop lying, do you, Emma?" he said softly. "I've only ever made the mistake of having Emma Ludgate as a girlfriend *once*," Dom said to me. "It's a mistake I wouldn't repeat if you paid me."

Emma was going bright red and I noticed her mouth quivering with rage. Dom continued to address me but made it perfectly clear it was for Emma's benefit.

"The problem with Emma is she's not only a liar, she's also extremely gullible. I mean, Carl started spreading this ridiculous story that I'd pretended to you that I had a rabbit called Beetroot and you'd believed me... But you'll never guess what – Emma believed him!"

"I *hate* you, Dominic Bede!" Emma said, stamping her foot like a six-year-old.

"It's good that we both feel the same way," Dom answered smoothly.

"I never want to set eyes on you again," she added.

"Perhaps I should go to Cableden School, then you wouldn't have to," Dom retorted. And with that he put his arm round my shoulders and kept it there until Emma had flounced off, trying to look as though she didn't care a jot, but failing.

The moment she'd gone, Dom removed his

arm and said, "You've every right to hate my guts, Jaimini. I came round here to apologize."

"I'm glad you're OK," I said truthfully. "Are you really leaving Finsbury?"

He nodded. "Everything I said just then was true except the bit about the rabbit..." He stopped and gave me a rather embarrassed look. I met his eyes and before we knew it we were both creased up, laughing.

"I've got to go," he said, straightening up. "I'll be seeing you soon, OK?"

"OK." But I didn't really think he would. That was just another of those things Dominic Bede couldn't help saying. I watched him saunter off and felt that perhaps I could face Mum by then.

Mum and Dad were both in the kitchen looking extraordinarily happy. That won't last, I thought miserably. Dad gave me a big hug and said, "Clever boyfriend you've got there. If it wasn't for his presence of mind, the police wouldn't have known where to start!"

"He's not actually my boyfriend, Dad," I told him.

"Oh, that's just a detail," Dad laughed.

Mum was laughing too. I had expected them to be relieved of course, but at the same time, very grave about the seriousness of not locking up, and the possible consequences. I was all prepared for a lecture on responsibility etc. I certainly hadn't expected this delirious happiness.

"Mum's got something to tell you," Dad informed me a moment later, with a twinkle in his eye.

I looked at Mum, and before she had said a single word, I suddenly knew what it was she had to tell me. But I couldn't be certain. I mustn't build up my hopes just in case I was wrong. I held my breath and waited.

"I'm pregnant!"

"*Yessssssssss!*" I gave her a massive hug, then gave Dad one, too. "Oh, that's brilliant. I'm going to have a baby brother or sister. *Mega!*"

"There's only one bad bit of timing," Mum said, with a big sigh.

"What's that?"

"My job. I wish I hadn't been so quick to go

back to work, especially as you're not even going to Finsbury now."

"You mean, you don't want your job?"

"It's the very last thing I want," she said, sadly.

"Well, don't worry, because you haven't got it!" I told her, laughing my head off.

"What do you mean…?"

They were both looking bewildered.

"A few days ago, when we were at our wits end about how to get me out of going to Finsbury, we had the brilliant idea that if you hadn't got a job, you wouldn't be able to afford the fees, so Andy found out who we should contact at the hospital, then Luce rang up St Prestlins, impersonating your voice, and told the woman there that you were very sorry for inconveniencing them, but you were afraid you couldn't now take the job, as your father had just died and your mother needed a lot of support… Apparently Sonja Davidson was most sympathetic and said you mustn't worry at all!"

Mum's eyes had gone from puzzled to

shocked to outraged while I'd been talking, and it was only as I finished that it suddenly occurred to me how much I had taken matters, which were really none of my business, into my own hands. I bit my lip and gave Mum a worried, apologetic look. There was a short silence while I grew more and more uncomfortable, then she totally threw me by breaking into a big smile.

"You naughty girl," she said slowly.

I took confidence from the smile and finished off my tale quickly and quietly.

"But when Luce phoned you, all prepared with her Sonja Davidson voice, there was no reply, and then we all completely forgot about it – until you phoned me in the café just now."

There followed a lot more hugging and then I tried to phone my friends to tell them the great news, but not *one* of them was in!

"Let's go for a walk," Mum suggested after a few minutes. "I could do with some fresh air."

"Very good for pregnant ladies," Dad joked.

We walked towards Cableden centre, and

after a bit I realized we were heading directly towards the café.

"Perhaps we should get something to eat?" Dad said. "I must say I'm feeling a bit peckish."

"Don't be silly, Dad. It'll be closed."

But I was wrong. All the lights were on and we could hear voices inside. Dad pushed open the door and I stood quite still in amazement. Jan had done the fastest transformation job any café has ever seen. The place was festooned with colour and all the tables were in a circle. But it wasn't that that had made me stop in my tracks, it was all the people, all cheering and letting off party poppers.

"Come on, Jaimini," Jan said, leading me to one of the tables. "This is the place for the star guest," and she led me to a place between Luce and Andy.

"Did you two know about this?" I asked Mum and Dad.

"We had a bit of an idea…" smiled Dad.

"But what's it all in aid of?" I asked.

"We're celebrating," Tash said.

"Good news spreads fast," Jan told me. Then she turned to Mum. "Congratulations. We're all so happy for you."

Mum and Dad looked as though they were going to burst with happiness, which was how I felt.

At that moment there was a faint tap on the door, and Jan suddenly looked a bit sheepish. "There was someone else I specially wanted to invite. I hope you don't mind, Jaimini."

Why should *I* mind? I wondered, but I understood what she meant when the door opened and in walked Dom. His eyes scanned the other faces, then rested on mine.

"I said I'd be seeing you soon," he said, then turning to Andy added, "I know I've got a lot of apologizing to do to Jaimini but I've made a good start, so I hope you approve."

"I don't mean to act like a mother hen," Andy laughed. "It's just that I don't like my friends getting hurt." Mum gave Andy a hug when she said that.

"I know you won't believe this," Dom went on, "but Carl and I had already agreed to drop the recording…"

"Why?" Luce demanded.

"I think Carl might like to tell you himself," Dom said.

"I'm sure he'd love to, but he can't because he's not here," Luce retorted.

"Well, actually," said Dom, walking towards the door. Then he flung it open and in walked Carl. He too looked rather shamefaced.

Luce stood up straight, put her hands on her hips, her head on one side and looked daggers at him. "I'm expecting a pretty big apology from you," she said in mock fury.

"But don't start yet," I added, joining in with the joke, "because we girls have got this competition going, and whoever gets the most recordings of boys grovelling to them, wins the competition!"

"Yes, OK. I get the message," Carl grinned sheepishly.

"Anyway, the reason we stopped recording was because we didn't care about the competition after a while." It was Dom who had spoken, but Carl nodded at his side. Luce for once was stuck for words. And so was I. This was the closest either of them had ever got to saying that they cared more about us than about the competition.

I had done a lot of growing up in one week, and I didn't know if Dom and I were to be boy and girlfriend or just good friends. All I knew was that whatever happened from now on would happen on *my* terms. I would call the tune.

"Oh, come on, you two," Jan said to Luce and me, seeing that neither of our expressions had softened one iota. "Surely you can forgive and forget now, can't you?"

Luce and I looked at each other.

"What do you think?" I asked her, in mock seriousness.

"I think we might just about forgive," she answered.

"But we won't forget, will we?" I stressed.

"Never," she agreed.

Carl and Dom looked at each other.

"I think *they* win," Carl said.

"I think you're right," Dom agreed.

"I'll drink to that," Andy announced, then Dad popped a Champagne cork and tipped the sparkling bubbly froth into everyone's glass.

"Here's to Dom," said Jan, raising her glass, "for bravery and quick thinking!"

"To Dom!" we all said.

"And here's to Jaimini, without whom the Café Club wouldn't be a Café Club!" cried Andy.

"To Jaimini," everybody echoed.

"And here's to baby Riva!" Luce carried on excitedly.

"Baby Riva!" came the answering cry.

"And let's hope it's a boy," said Tash, with feeling.

A very knowing look passed between Luce and me.

"No, let's hope it's a girl," we said, at exactly the same moment.

Join

Would you and your friends like to know more about Fen, Tash, Leah, Andy, Jaimini and Luce?

We have produced a special bookmark to commemorate the launch of the Café Club series. To get yours free, together with a special newsletter about Fen and her friends, their creator, author Ann Bryant, and advance information about what's coming next in the series, write (enclosing a self-addressed label, please) to:

The Café Club
c/o the Publicity Department
Scholastic Children's Books
Commonwealth House
1-19 New Oxford Street
London WC1A 1NU

We look forward to hearing from you!

Goosebumps

by R.L. Stine

Reader beware, you're in for a scare!

These terrifying tales will send shivers up your spine . . .

Available now:

Hippo Fantasy

Lose yourself in a whole new world, a world where anything is possible – from wizards and dragons, to time travel and new civilizations . . . Gripping, thrilling, scary and funny by turns, these Hippo Fantasy titles will hold you captivated to the very last page.

The Night of Wishes
Michael Ende (author of *The Neverending Story*)

Malcolm and the Cloud-Stealer
Douglas Hill

The Wednesday Wizard
Sherryl Jordan

Ratspell
Paddy Mounter

Rowan of Rin
Emily Rodda

The Practical Princess
Jay Williams

*If you like animals, then you'll love
Hippo Animal Stories!*

Look out for:

Animal Rescue by Bette Paul

Tessa finds life in the country *so* different from life in
the town. Will she ever be accepted? But everything
changes when she meets Nora and Ned who run the
village animal sanctuary, and becomes involved in a
struggle to save the badgers of Delves Wood
from destruction . . .

Thunderfoot by Deborah van der Beek

Mel Whitby has always loved horses, and when she
comes across an enormous by neglected horse in a
railway field, she desperately wants to take care of it.
But little does she know that taking care of
Thunderfoot will change her life forever . . .

A Foxcub Named Freedom
by Brenda Jobling

A vixen lies seriously injured in the undergrowth. Her
young son comes to her for comfort and warmth. The
cub wants to help his mother to safety, but it is
impossible. The vixen, sensing danger, nudges him
away, caring nothing for herself – only for
his freedom . . .